Danger on the Trail

And there Rube was with nothing! Shadow had not only taken his horse, he had taken the saddle and bedroll with his tarp and blankets, his saddlebags with all his chuck and stuff, even the Winchester. Everything a man depends on was trapped on that mare—and now gone, except for his lariat and his revolver, which had fallen in the snow.

Sighing, groaning, he gathered up his horsehair rope and bit at the throbbing place on his finger. Then he started out, kicking rocks as he hiked down the gorge rim. He carried his lariat slung over one shoulder and his .44 in his hand.

He shivered, sore and lonely and tied in knots from the grief of it all—yes, and angry too, so mad and sick and sorry that he didn't mind going hungry for a while, except that he knew that'd make it easier to freeze to death. And just then, when everything looked like it couldn't get worse, he saw riders in the dim evening ahead.

They were Indians.

QUANTITY SALES

Galloping Wind

---

by Zoltan Malocsay

A DELL BOOK

Published by
Dell Publishing
a division of
The Bantam Doubleday Dell Publishing Group, Inc.
1 Dag Hammarskjold Plaza
New York, New York 10017

Dell ® TM 681510, Dell Publishing, a division of the Bantam Doubleday Dell Publishing Group, Inc.

ISBN: 0-440-20138-1

Printed in the United States of America
Published simultaneously in Canada
June 1988
10 9 8 7 6 5 4 3 2 1

OPM

To Dolores, Eloese, Meredyth, and Vivian

Acknowledgments

I'd like to acknowledge the special help and encouragement of Stanley Pashko and Ellen Small, former Fiction Editors of *Boy's Life* magazine, who helped me develop the original short story version of *Galloping Wind*, published in October of 1973.

Lynn Wilson, Bianca Maniaci, and Don Beebe of Boulder, Colorado, lent their special knowledge of mustangs and mountain ranching. Background material came from several factual books, but, most of all, *Galloping Wind* was inspired by the historical accounts of real mustangs in J. Frank Dobie's *The Mustangs*.

Chapter 1

———— ◆◆ ————

Rube pretended he didn't see the dark shape passing in the pines up above. He tried to rein back some, to hold back without looking obvious, while his pa and the other mustangers charged on by with whistles and shouts, driving wild horses down the canyon toward a snare they had built at the other end. Any second now that rail fence trap would boil with wild horses, but Rube had to wonder about the one on the ridge, that black shadow moving in the trees up there.

It was a stallion, watching, following, curious to know what was happening, but careful not to get too close. Rube couldn't get a proper look, what with the snow-dressed greenery screening him and all, but he knew he was there, knew it sure, the same way some folks can see fish in the water where others can't. It's just a feel you get after chasing something all your life.

Rube Tucker was seventeen that October of 1896. It was a bright, snowy afternoon just glistening for the chase, and even after a week's hard riding he didn't want to see it end. Anyway not before he got a better look at that spy on the ridge, that "Shadow."

When the wild ones hit the trap ahead, it was all shouts and whistles and yahooing to keep them in, while lariats snaked out to catch the picket gates. Once those picket gates dragged over and closed the pen, things just about got warm because mustangs have the notion that any horse should be able to break out of any corral, if he goes about it crazy enough.

But they were in, by golly, a whirlpool of steam-breathing wild ones, all bumping and crashing around. "Hey, Pa!" Rube shouted over the noise. When his pa turned, Rube nodded toward the ridge. "I'm going after one up there!"

Seth heard him just well enough to nod in a distracted sort of way, so Rube reined out fast. He had to kick Red several times to break her attention, but once he had her pointed up that ridge and she caught sight of what they were after, she broke into a dash all her own, anxious for the chase again.

That flushed the stallion. He broke from the timber and topped the ridge at a clear space. He whirled there with a toss of his head that sent his black mane flying like spray, shining, while he hurled an open-throated whinny at the mares he had hidden on the other side.

For that one heart-stopping second, Rube had a good look, a vivid picture to haunt him always. He was blue-black, that stallion, a deep black that sheened to blue in the sun like the barrel of a new rifle. He had four stocking feet, clean white to the knee, all even, and a long star on his face that didn't reach his nose.

He wasn't the biggest stallion in the world—his breed never are—but his legs were long and slender and made him look tall just the same. Yet his head proved his blood: he was Arabian, Spanish Barb really, the kind of horse the conquistadors rode centuries back. No other breed has such a delicate, refined look, with a head that tapers down to a muzzle so tiny that it could fit into a coffee cup.

Here was a kind of horse Rube had only seen in pictures, in magazines like *Harper's Weekly*, with a flowing-gowned sheik or an armored conquistador on his back. The same stock had been running wild for centuries, but only rarely did that quality show. This was a throwback, a mountain jewel born in the image of his ancestors. His pa always said there might be one, maybe one, somewhere up in the Winding Stair peaks. In places like that, in remote places untouched and forgotten, Nature sorts for the best in any breed.

And here he was, the kind of horse mustangers only dream about. Rube had a throat with a lump and a mouth without words, just that kind of wide-eyed wonder that leaves you too stunned to do much of anything. If it hadn't been for Red carrying him up that ridge, he might have just sat there frozen, like some hunters get when they see the perfect shot and can't move.

But old Red was going, her eyes tied to that spot on the ridge, her nostrils full of the chase she loved. Up that slope she went in hard, jarring lurches, then down the other side with snow rolling after.

The trees hid Shadow from sight for a minute, but the tracks were plain and Red needed no kind of reining. Not her. She made it scary! It was all Rube could do to sit her, what with snow-laden branches flapping past, and she tree-dodging like a rabbit, slanting hard from side to side.

When they reached a meadow, he got a glimpse of Shadow and his band of sixteen mares and older colts. Then he followed them up again, up and up some more, then down into a little valley, five or six miles or better. He lost all track.

Which was dumb, really. He knew that Pa and the

others would be waiting back at Squaw Canyon. It was getting on toward dusk, too, and he sure didn't hold out much hope of catching that stallion all by himself, but somehow none of that mattered. He just wasn't ready to stop and watch that beautiful black gallop away. Rube was a mustanger, plain and simple, and for all he knew this might be the last great stallion he'd ever see, maybe the last one of his quality left in the West. He had a mighty hunger for just one more look—and then another and another.

He followed Shadow and his manada up to the gorge of Roaring River in the foothills of the Winding Stairs. They climbed up to that canyon crack where it gets most narrow, up to that gap where it makes you dizzy to look down. Then the stallion signaled for his lead mare to take the others across.

That meant jump a place where the swallows sail far below, where the river's roar is all but lost in the wind and the distance. Jump that! Rock to rock!

The lead mare was a calico pony with a white splotch over one eye, a wise old gal who followed orders without a blink and who gave some orders of her own. With no hesitation at all she ran to the edge and leaped.

The sight of it made Rube catch his breath, for a blast of wind from way below took her mane and tail flying, just seemed to lift her in the air. She made it look so easy that the first several after her tried it with no fear. Like woolies over a fence, one, two, three, four, and then the fifth one missed her footing at the edge. Her head ducked, she faltered, but she was way too close to back away, so she tried it anyhow—and missed.

Her forefeet clipped the far edge but didn't have the footing to pull her on. Her back hooves never touched at all, and, when a scream that tore at your insides, she vanished out of sight. Three hundred feet to Roaring River.

That put a fear in those that followed, but Shadow was there, kicking and biting at backsides, whinnying his order over and over again, because with every toss of his head, he could see Rube and old Red coming. The lead mare bared her teeth with a whinny to back him up, and they jumped all right. One after another, just like before, the rest of the mares leaped over until only Shadow was left on this side.

Lariat in hand now, Rube bore down on him just as fast as Red could go. Yet now the stallion paused. He paused and then he pranced out toward Rube, neck arched, nostrils flaring, almost like he was fixing to fight.

Still charging, Rube blinked and swallowed. What do I do if I rope him? He'll kill me! Yet the stallion was there to be roped and the rope was already circling. Everything in him craved to try. He just couldn't imagine stopping now.

Shadow snorted steam and pawed the ground, but when Rube and Red didn't slow, he whirled suddenly and made for the gap.

Rube's lariat whooshed around and around. Almost close enough.

Shadow tucked in his chin as he charged to the edge. Then he gathered his legs under him and he sprang.

Rube threw—too late. The rope brushed Shadow's back, its loop closing near the flick of his tail. Flinty black hooves clicked rocks on the other side, and he was safe.

The dizzy dream busted then, and Rube was almost glad. He wrenched back rein and stood back in the stirrups, turning Red near the edge. They went round and round there, she too excited to stop.

Rube looked to the other ledge and saw the stallion

looking back. That's when he made his promise, a promise that someday he'd have that stallion, not just to break and sell like the others, but have him for his very own.

Shadow reared up high and shook his head, as if meaning to say that it would never be so. And oh what a picture he made there on that rock, pawing at the purple-orange sky, his mane in the wind like rippling silk. The best of the best and free to any man who could take him.

"Someday you're mine," Rube whispered.

That was the promise he made at Roaring River Gorge, and even at the time Shadow was daring him to make that promise good. He just dared Rube to jump that gap and deal with him on the other side.

"Whoa, there, whoa!" He had to keep Red from trying, too, the loco cuss. She'd never make it over that chasm, not with him and a saddle and a bedroll and all.

Shadow backed away from the edge, and Rube started to do the same. He had one hand full of jumpy horse and the other hand full of tangled rope, when suddenly he heard hooves on rock again. Looking up, he saw Shadow coming, charging straight for the chasm again!

His legs made a pliers grip flinch around Red, and his hands started fumbling with the rope. Too late, he realized that he should have run!

Shadow jumped the gap and came straight at him, his ears laid back, his mouth open, his teeth bared.

Rube's eyes went wide, his heels came down into Red's sides, every muscle trying to get that horse around and going. Oh, she was going all right, shying back and twisting, but the stallion was coming faster.

"Hey-ah!" he yelled, flaying to go. Red launched herself into a run, but Shadow had speed and he was on them like a trout after a fly.

Rube couldn't look where he was going. All he could

see were those jaws opening, those white teeth coming
for him—*wolf teeth!* He had those extra teeth that rare
stallions grow in the wild sometimes. They were meat-
tearing teeth, like a wolf's, sharper, a little longer than
his others. They were in those spaces where a bridle bit
should go, the spaces called "the bars." Here was a horse
never born for a bridle, a horse so wild for so many genera-
tions that he drew from the past a throwback trait dating
to prehistoric days.

Those nostrils blew steam, the black lips curled back,
the wolf teeth aimed for Rube himself. At the last instant
Rube leaned in the saddle, trying to duck, but those fangs
followed right on in toward his arm. He tucked back his
arm, squinted to feel the teeth closing. His arm found
room to flinch somewhere just as those jaws chop-clopped
shut on his jacket, so the horse bit leather and not his arm.

Then came the yank. Red was going, but Shadow just
stiffened his forelegs like a roping horse fixing to yank
down a steer. The jerk almost pulled Rube's arm out of
socket. He flipped backwards out of the saddle, and
Shadow let go then, letting him fall. He hit the ground
rolling and thought he saw Shadow's hooves in flight
over him.

He saw those hooves going over and right there he
put "Amen" to all his prayers because he couldn't outrun
that stallion on his hands and knees, and that's what it
was down to. He flopped over and tried, of course, sure
that any second those hind hooves would fire into him like
a double-barreled shotgun. He scrambled a few yards, put
his hand into a snow-covered cactus doing it and got a
spine deep in the third finger of his left hand, but kept
going, waiting for death to come and mash him.

Everything behind him was noise and fury, hooves on
rock and whinnies and all. *Red's sticking up for me!* he

thought. *Maybe she'll give me enough time to get away.* Oh, he loved that mare that instant, prayed for her to give a good fight.

He made a few yards' distance and glanced back. Red and Shadow were going around and around, all fury, with Shadow nipping at her behind and Red all white-eyed with panic. She tripped on one of her reins, broke it, and then Shadow choppered down on her hard. With a whinny, she flinched straight forward and when his teeth came for her again, she ducked her head, made a short run to the edge, and then sprang for all she was worth. Saddle, bridle, and all, she leaped Roaring River Gorge.

It wasn't until that instant that Rube realized he was being robbed!

Shadow didn't even look at him lying there bewildered on the ground. He just leaped after his prize and went to herd her in with the rest of his mares.

There on the other side Red turned and looked Rube's way, a pitiful look, a lot scared and a little sorry. Helpless is what it was. It was just a glance that she gave him, but it was a farewell long enough to remember always.

Then Shadow gave her a nudge and she went off with them, looking mighty strange with her man-carrying gear strapped on all over.

"Red!" he called, but then he stopped, knowing it was too late. He panted steam. He was worn out, cold, and cactus-stuck, bleeding from hand and heart, not even standing because he hadn't had time to get up yet, just halfway crouch-kneeling there, watching them go, and Red with them. The best mustanging mare he'd ever owned, stolen right out from under him—by a mustang no less!—and herded off now with the rest of the manada to become a mustang herself. He wondered then how she'd fare with all that tack strapped on. How would she ever get rid of that stuff?

As for Shadow—well, he had the cussed gall not to even look back. So Rube stood up then, just as they were near out of sight, and he hollered to the wind that followed them, "That's a loan, by thunder! I'll have her back and you, too, you, you—"

He ran out of breath then and just watched till the moment came when they were gone out of sight and he was left there by himself on the rim of Roaring River Gorge. The sky yawned big all around, darkening fast in the east, bluer and bluer, while the oranges that colored the fast-running clouds over west got dimmer and dimmer. The big mountains were getting ready for bed and there he was, alone and afoot near the Winding Stairs.

You just can't imagine how a horse-riding man can feel when he finds himself afoot someplace so far away, with nothing or nobody around to help and dark coming on, with all that means. A horse is such company to a man— even if you happen not to like the cuss—that, well, being suddenly alone, really alone, can be so strange and unfamiliar.

Too, he had good reason to be worried. October nights in the Winding Stairs are no joke. The wind keens high and drives the cold through your clothes like needles. Men have died. Even with all the gear they should have had, men had died from snowbound nights in the Winding Stairs.

And there he was with nothing! Shadow had not only taken his horse, he had taken the saddle and bedroll with his tarp and blankets, his saddlebags with all his chuck and stuff, even the Winchester. Everything a man depends on was strapped to that mare—and now gone, except for his lariat and his revolver, which had fallen in the snow.

Sighing, groaning, he gathered up his horsehair rope and bit at the throbbing place on his finger. Then he started out, kicking rocks as he hiked down the gorge rim. He carried his lariat slung over one shoulder and his .44 in his hand just in case supper jumped into its muzzle. Rube never was much of a shot with a handgun, you see, and there was never a weapon less well designed for supper-killing.

He shivered, sore and lonely and tied in knots from the grief of it all—yes, and angry too, so mad and sick and sorry that he didn't mind going hungry for awhile, except that he knew that'd make it easier to freeze to death. And just then, when everything looked like it couldn't get worse, he saw riders in the dim evening ahead.

They were Indians.

Chapter 2

◆ ◆ ◆

Rube guessed he might have cashed in right there if it hadn't been for those Indians. Chevals they were, from up near the Cloud Cascades, and they were down here doing just what he was doing, mustanging.

Pa always said the Chevals were the best mustangers in the northwest Rockies. French trappers named the tribe after marveling at the way they handled horses. The word *cheval*, which is pronounced like "shove ALL," means *horse* in French, so the Chevals were the Horse tribe.

Old Roki was their eldest mustanger and he led the outfit. He and Pa had been friends for years, and Rube grew up gnawing on one of those turtleshell rattles the Indians make.

Roki was the original salt-jerked and dried-in-the-sun mustanger, the kind of crazy old man who will never quit. He was half-blind without his spectacles—big eight-sided oval things, gold wire around thin glass—but he managed to ride some rough places with the earpieces tied behind his head. His hair was white, bound into long braids down his shoulders. He wore leather and calico clothes and a pair of cavalry boots that he won in a horserace, and he rode a Mexican saddle with a horn as big as a saucer. Part of the saddle had just a bare wood tree, with no leather on it at all, but it must've suited Roki's old bones just fine.

With him was his grandson, Kehoni, a silent kid maybe a year younger than Rube. He hadn't met Kehoni but once before when he had been lots younger. Now Kehoni looked hard and brown, bundled up and ready for the trail.

Three other braves were Roki's usual mustanger crew, but the outfit did include a fourth old Indian Rube had never seen before. The others treated him with extra respect, and he didn't seem outfitted like a regular mustanger, though he handled himself comfortably enough on horseback. Later on, Rube found out that he was their shaman, or medicine man.

They all got a right old laugh when they found out why Rube was afoot. All except Kehoni, who didn't seem to think it was so funny. They seemed to be laughing at Kehoni, too.

Kehoni fixed Rube with an anxious look. "Did—did the black one have a mare, a pinto?" He pointed to his left eye, then his right shoulder. "A pinto with white here and here?"

Rube nodded. "She was leading."

"Leading!" Roki laughed, as Kehoni's face darkened. Roki translated to the others who didn't speak as much English and they all laughed and went on in Cheval about things Rube didn't understand. Kehoni just seemed to wither up and bear it.

"You see, Kehoni?" Roki grinned. "The Spirit takes from all of us."

Rube frowned. "That—that wasn't your pinto, was it?"

Kehoni didn't even answer, the others were ribbing him so. His lips just got tighter and tighter.

Rube felt awful sorry for him, of course, but in a way he felt relieved to share some of the ribbing with him. Seemed like neither of them could be blamed so much, since the culprit made such a regular practice of stealing saddlehorses right out from under folks.

"The shaman says you should be flattered," Roki went on at Kehoni. "He says she must be a fine mare, if the Wind-That-Gallops has her leading."

"Wind-That-Gallops," Rube said. "Is that what you call him?"

Roki nodded and held up two fingers. "For two winters I chase him. One winter he is too young to have a manada of his own, and now he has some of my best mares!" He thumped his chest with his fingers. "My best mares!"

Rube squinted up into the mountains' last light. "Well, you'll get 'em back," he said, all grit and confidence.

Roki gave him the darnedest look then, a long, slow look, smiling very gently, like a pat on the head, a wordless way of blessing him for being so young and foolish. Which made Rube feel right uncomfortable, but there was no use pushing. Besides, presently Roki and the others started seeing to his comfort in other ways, so he let it pass.

They took him to a sheltered place under an overhanging rock, and there they made camp for the night. They made a fire and roasted up a rabbit that Hand-in-the-Fire had killed, but that only made a taste all around and not the kind of meal you lay into after riding all day in the snow. So the rest of it was just jerked meat and melted snow.

Sure did feel strange sitting there on the ground with

not even a saddle to prop under his arm. No blanket, nothing but his horsehair lariat. But at least his friends were generous and came fitted for the night they had coming.

They circled up close around a tiny campfire, each of them taking turns squinting and face-tossing in the smoke. The wind kept beating around from many directions so that somebody was always getting a little cured. Far away was the rush of Roaring River, and all around came the changing pitch of wind in the trees and rocks, at times a kind of whine. Smoke or no smoke, they were glad to sit close around that fire.

Of course, for a while there his friends didn't have much to say to each other, though it was more a matter of that jerky keeping their jaws busy.

Rube watched old Roki in the firelight. The yellow light that wavered with the wind made his face and arms look strange, all tough and sinewy, worn and sunbrowned, kinda like the jerky they were eating. It looked as if dried meat was going from mouth to muscle straight off, with no more effort than it took to chew up and swallow the stuff, which was considerable effort at that.

Rube used the time to think and dream and scheme about Shadow, about how to catch him and how to get Red back. The obvious answer was for all of them to pull together and see what they could do tomorrow, but the big black hole in that idea was knowing that Roki might catch Shadow first. Old Roki was a talent; Pa always said so. He'd roped a lot of mustangs, and if all of them had the same chance, Roki'd likely be the one to make it.

For a moment there Rube got all edgy and worried, then felt downright ashamed of himself for being so afraid that a friend might have a little good luck and catch the horse he wanted. That'd never happened between their peoples before, between any mustanger and the Tucker family, because the land was always so wide and open and full that there always seemed to be enough to go around for all those who had the guts to go out looking. He never thought that he and Roki could get crowded together chasing the same horse, and what made him feel even worse was knowing that it wasn't Roki who was causing this problem.

Roki wasn't horning in on him. If anything, it was the other way around. After all, Roki had seen the stallion first, named him, chased him for two years, even lost mares to him. By all rights, Rube figured he should back off and let Roki have him, but he couldn't do that. The very thought made his insides whine.

So he bit down hard on his salt-dried jerky, bit like maybe it could take some of the pain and frustration of it all. A mouthful of snowmelt helped him work up a beefy juice, but as he swallowed, he had to wonder if Roki wasn't thinking the same thing—wishing that he'd go away and leave the stallion to him.

"Old friend," Rube started, almost as if they were the same age, "I don't recollect us ever chasing the same horse before."

Roki studied him, as if looking for some other meaning. "There are many wild horses."

"Not so many any more, not really fine ones."

Hand-in-the-Fire made a noise like that was so, but Roki said nothing.

"You say the stallion comes from up your way?"

Roki shook his head. "No, he comes from away toward there." His arm gestured wide. "From the high meadows of the Winding Stairs."

Rube let his eyes wander away toward that direction. Even though he couldn't see anything but darkness, he looked toward the Winding Stairs and his imagination sailed. For that nest of mountain peaks had always fascinated him; it was a special place "good for nothing but scenery," as Pa liked to say. It wasn't far, but mighty hard to get to. He'd only been there twice before, and the place was so high and rugged that even the Indians wouldn't try to live there on any regular basis.

"Most always he is there," Roki said. "He only comes to the Cloud Cascades to steal my horses."

Rube shared his joke with a smile, and then he waited a long, tense moment. "I was just wondering if you lay any kind of claim to him, because we've been friends a long time and—" Everybody looked so puzzled that he ran out of steam.

Rube shook his head and tried to explain. "See, you've been chasing him so long that I thought you might—well, I want that horse so bad I don't know if I can sleep tonight."

Roki and the others traded smiles at that one. "He is a beautiful horse," Roki said, "but you will get used to not having him. I have."

"But if you catch him before I can," Rube asked, almost wanting to hold his breath, "would you sell him to me?"

Everything got real quiet, for he had just opened up a whole Indian ritual, the horse trade. Roki thought on it for a moment while beside him the shaman began to hum a little chant to himself, way down low.

Rube waited, his thumb and forefinger rubbing together a pinch of pantcloth at a fold. Finally, old Roki shook his head. "We should not talk on this while the black one is gone in the mountains. Besides, we will never catch him."

"Why not? I mean, if you don't, I sure plan to."

Roki allowed himself just the smallest hint of a smile, but the others grinned a little bigger and the medicine man stopped chanting. "You have strong hopes," Roki told him.

"Strong dreams. I tell you as a friend: don't hurt yourself. You don't know this Wind-That-Gallops."

Rube tucked back his chin and made a puzzled face.

"There are many wild ones," Roki told him very softly. "You can have many. Don't break your heart wanting just this one."

"Well, you want him, don't you?"

Roki nodded sharply. "Yes, but I know we will never catch him. Ever."

"Why not? I mean, you go to the trouble of chasing him—"

"He is strong medicine, Rube Tucker. Strong medicine." Roki's voice had a hint of warning in it.

Rube wrinkled up his forehead, puzzled, as the nod of heads drew his gaze from Indian to Indian. "Strong medicine," he said. "What's that mean?"

"More than I can say." Roki shrugged. "But I don't think that any man can catch him. Ever."

Rube was in no mood to hear that, not after losing his best mare and all. "I've caught a lot of mustangs." He snorted.

"Yes, but only horses."

Rube screwed up one eye at that one. "Well, what are we talking about, then?"

"Maybe—" Roki shrugged. "Maybe the one you call Shadow is not a horse at all. My shaman says he is not." His gaze flicked toward the medicine man when he said that, the shaman now humming that low song again, eyes closed, lost in it.

Rube leaned a little closer toward Roki, his voice low. "Well, uh, what, uh . . . what does he say he is, then?"

The shaman's song changed pitch, going higher, so Roki waited until it swung low again before speaking up. "You name him rightly, this Shadow. A thing you see, but cannot touch. You can chase, but never catch. My shaman says he is a spirit, a—a gust of wind that wears a horse's skin."

"Well, he wears a horse's teeth too!" Rube showed him the arm of his jacket. "His bite's sure real enough."

"Oh, I did not say that he is not real! Even spirits are real. Don't you think that spirits are real?"

Rube shrugged, not wanting to get into that.

Roki leaned back, looking amazed. "Don't you think that spirits are real?"

Rube tried shrugging again, not knowing what to say. Like everybody, Indians have their own ideas about things, and he didn't want to step on another man's beliefs. But old Roki sat there waiting for an answer until he had to say something. "Well, I don't know much about those things, Roki. I just don't know how real spirits are. I never stubbed my toe on one—"

Roki laughed, then rubbed at the air with his hand. "No, no. We talk of, of—" He made a hard fist— "of will, of life, of all those things you will not stub your toe on. You have felt the power of a mustang fighting at your rope—"

Rube nodded.

"You have seen the fire in his eyes." He touched his own eyes. "They flame with a will very strong, very proud."

"Sure."

"And also you have seen that flame go out." He made a snatching motion, then snapped his fingers. "You have seen that fire die in his eyes."

"You mean like when you break a horse, that look in his eyes?"

Roki bobbed his head. "One day he is chief of the mountains, with fire and pride in his eyes, and in another day—"

"His spirit's broke." Rube nodded, finally understanding. "I see. You mean 'horse spirit.' Sure, I know what 'spirited' horses are and, sure, you've gotta break some of that 'spirit' or you can't even ride 'em. I thought you were talking about something—something strange."

Roki looked surprised. "You don't think that's strange?"

"Well, no. It's just . . . natural."

"But not strange?"

"All right, all right. Come to think of it, I reckon a lot of things natural are strange, but I thought you were talking about ghosts or something."

"Maybe so," Roki said, and he didn't look as if he was funning, either, which worried Rube all over again.

"I—uh—thought we were talking about 'horse spirit.' "

Roki nodded surely. "When that flame goes out, where does it go? It was there, real as life. Then gone. Surely you have seen it, the fire this Shadow has. When you saw him close, could you not see that he is more than just a good horse? I have never seen him really close like you, but even with these old eyes, I can see that he is somehow . . . special."

Rube looked to the others and found himself swallowing the knowledge that Shadow had struck him that way, too. That first glimpse hit him so hard that the picture was still nailed in his mind. Yes, he was special all right, in ways he couldn't say, and it gave him a strange feeling, sitting here talking to another man who felt the same way.

The wind howled up behind him, making him shiver and pull himself tense within his coat. The wind made the campfire wash around fluttering, its smoke streaming over the shaman now, who folded up like a flower bud with his head tucked down between his knees.

Roki gazed into the fire for a long moment. "I hope

someday I can see him as close as you have, but even at a distance I can see—" His spectacles flashed when he lifted his gaze from the fire. "In some way I do not know, Rube Tucker, this Shadow burns with a fire very old, very strong. I have broken many horses, seen the light go out in their eyes, but somehow, somehow he has gathered it all up, all that spirit of all the wild ones. He has gathered it up, and it makes him strong. It makes him proud and beautiful and wild."

Rube found himself nodding before he was even through thinking it over. Maybe it was just the campfire and the wind and the night and all the talk about mountain spirits, but a spooky feeling crept over him. He found himself looking behind him, even though there was nothing out there.

Wait a minute, he thought, we're talking about mustangs, not spooks. "All you say has truth to it, Roki, but I'm still going to catch him. Spirit or no spirit, he's still horse enough to rope."

"Maybe so," Roki agreed, "but I don't think we can catch him."

He said it gentlelike, but Rube found it hard not to be ruffled. "Why not?"

"You will see," Roki sighed. "A mountain spirit with no saddle and no man on his back can run many places where you cannot follow."

Rube simmered slowly. Here he was being told that he might as well not bother chasing the best wild horse in the mountains, and here being told that by another mustanger who was out chasing that very horse himself. "Roki, if you don't think I should bother going after this stallion, then why are you out chasing him?"

Roki shook his head. "Rube Tucker," he scolded gently,

"I never said I could catch him, either. We only chase him."

Rube squinted. "Only chase him!"

Roki bobbed his head, as did others.

"All this way?"

Roki nodded again.

"What for? I mean, well, yeah—what for?"

Roki unclasped his hands long enough to raise his fingers in a shrugging motion. "Why did you chase him? You had no chance alone. You knew you could not catch him."

Rube struggled to spill out some reason, but Roki had him. "Well, I—I don't know, I guess, except . . . I saw him and I wanted to see him closer. Heck, I'm a mustanger! I chase wild horses. That's what I do."

Roki nodded real slow. "It is strong medicine just to chase him. Just to follow him over the land for a time is very close to all things wild and free and beautiful."

"But are you saying you wouldn't throw a loop if you got the chance?"

Roki smiled away his question. "I am a mustanger, too, Rube Tucker. We make medicine by chasing him, but if I got the chance, I would have to try for him." He motioned toward Rube's lariat. "Maybe I will make a magic rope like yours."

"This?" Rube picked it up.

At that, the shaman spoke quickly to Roki in Cheval, a short question, and Roki nodded. "He has heard of your rope and would like to hold it."

Rube looked at the medicine man and wondered, then he handed over his prize horsehair rope. The shaman opened his palms with a real reverence.

Roki gestured toward the rope. "With your own hands,

you have woven together hairs from all the ponies you ever loved, all the ponies you ever held as yours. Such a thing can be strong medicine. With such a rope, you might catch a mountain spirit. But you would have to be very close, and that's your problem."

Rube didn't know what to make of his strong medicine talk, but he was right about the rope's being good enough to do the job. It was a darned good rope. He'd worked on it since he was five or six, and he had made it just right. At first, he kept doing it just to remember the horses of his life, thinning their tails and saving the hair. But in Rube's line of work, a fellow can enjoy a lot of horses, and after awhile the rope got long, long enough to use. No use leaving it on the mantelpiece back at the ranch. He'd rather have it with him— oh, there's nothing like a good horsehair rope!—and if he wanted it on the mantelpiece, he could always have it there when he was home to see it.

The shaman studied the lariat, held it like it was pure gold, which is just about the way Rube felt about it himself. Then the medicine man nodded approvingly to Roki and handed it back, all with due respect, while he let flow some of that beautiful jabber of theirs. Roki translated. "He says it has the feel of magic, much love and care and closeness. Medicine very strong. He also says that you could have made more closeness by weaving in your own hairs, too." Roki laced his fingers together as he said it. "You and the horse, together in the rope."

Rube dipped his head to one side in a shrugging motion. "Well, like you say, if I'm good enough to get close, it's good enough to hold the stallion."

"Just don't tie your happiness to a dream," Roki warned. "Your dream might run away with it."

"I plan to hang on real tight," Rube grunted, scooting back to where he could stretch out his legs. Everybody was making motions toward sleep. "I just want to get an early start come sunup. I want to catch Red before something happens to my Winchester and stuff."

"I hope so," Roki said.

"Ought to be easy." Rube wrapped the blankets tighter around himself and squirmed to get comfortable on his bed of pine boughs. "She'll come if she sees me."

"I hope so," came another voice, Kehoni's this time. He was lying there on one arm, across the fire where Rube could still see his face. He looked so sad it made you hurt, his eyes far off in a way that looked near tears. "My Firelight," he said, "she would always come when I called her. Always." He rolled over then, face to the dark. "But no more. No more."

Rube pursed his brows, wondering on that. "You mean to say you got close enough to call her and she wouldn't come?"

Kehoni didn't answer, but in the dim light Rube could barely see the shake of his head.

"You mean she wouldn't come to you?"

Again he shook his head. "She forgot me like a stranger." His whisper had tears in it some place. "And she was only gone two days."

Two days! Rube frowned, now suddenly afraid that Red might—but no! Red used to be wild, sure, but that was years ago, three years ago. Now she was trained, trained to hunt wild horses, not be a wild horse. A couple of nights in the Winding Stairs couldn't make her forget all that.

Could it?

He rolled over one way, then the other, trying to find

an arrangement of lumps that fit his body better. And the whole time his body seemed to split into two parts, his head that was sure that Red would come when he called her and his stomach that was wound in knots from being unsure. "Kehoni, how long'd you have that pony before Shadow took her?"

He watched the dark lump stir beyond the campfire. Kehoni hesitated a long moment before he answered. "Four summers," he said. "I had her more than four summers."

Chapter 3

———— ◆◆ ————

Rube had a hard time sleeping that night, what with the wind pulling his thoughts away like smoke from a campfire, making his fears and his dreams sail off down the canyons, maybe even toward the place where Shadow stood on guard.

Worry and want rolled him back and forth like meat on a griddle, first the worry that he wouldn't get Red back, then the pure star-gazing want for the blue-black stallion, then the worry that he wouldn't get him after all, which led him straight back to worrying about Red again. And so it went until he got to worrying about whether or not he'd get any sleep.

Morning came none too soon. It was a pretty morning, with the sun's rays slanting through the snow-laden trees, glittering there like scatterings of diamonds in the drifts. It was that kind of morning that made him feel weak and foolish for grumbling at it like a bear. Hand-in-the-Fire gave him some jerky, and Rube didn't know which was more cold and stiff, himself or that jerky, but he ate it just to prove he was more alive than it was and because he knew it was the only breakfast he was going to get.

Then they repacked all the supplies they had left, putting some on each horse, so as to free the packhorse they had along. Rube rode the packhorse bareback. Crazy as he was to catch Red and Shadow, he wasn't crazy enough to try it bareback on that packhorse. That pony had a spine like a razorback hog. Like a railsplitter's wedge, it was honed to a sharpness that could split a man up between the ears.

As soon as they got to the bottom of the gorge, he let Roki and the rest go on while he rode off to find Pa's camp. He figured he could get another mount, then reprovision this packhorse and meet up with Roki up beyond the gorge. But he didn't count on bad luck.

As he rode into camp, he met Russian Will, who gave him all the bad news in that tongue-rolling drawl of his. Will was Russian all right, had come over when he was about twenty. Will's folks settled in Texas, so that was where he learned his English, Texas cowtalk pronounced with a Russian roll.

He was a barrel-chested fellow with short legs and a fuzzy beard that spread like gray-blue sagebrush all around his face. He wore a black felt hat without a dent or a fold in it anyplace, wore it tugged down over the top of his sagebrush to shade his eyes. He talked a lot with his hands.

It seemed all fury had cut loose after Rube left them. Herb Fincher, one of Pa's regulars, broke an arm trying to keep back mustangs while the boys mended a break in the gate. Two of their sixteen head got away through the break, and one of them dragged down Joe Simpson's horse and broke the girth on his saddle.

That left them shy a saddle as well as a rider, not counting Rube, and all at a time when they had fourteen wild mustangs and one busted mustanger to get home. That was hard, for no matter how weak and worn out those mustangs were, they still had a chance of getting away on the trail drive home.

Pa never liked to string his catch together with ropes the way they did some places because there was so much timber that their mustangs would only tangle up and choke and then fight to kill anybody who tried to help. Sometimes they would keep a rope on a lead mare or tie a prize horse to an old mule, but generally they drove herds of this size—stampeded them!—with men on every side, keeping them spooked every second.

That worked because the wild ones got so scared that their herding instinct took over. Instead of scattering, they huddled close and ran as a group. It would take every man and every saddlehorse to keep those mustangs spooked, to keep that stampede under control. If Rube didn't stay to help, they'd be shy two men instead of one, and that would surely cost them horses. Some would get away.

Sighing, Rube pressured the nag with his knees so as to relieve the pressure elsewhere, and guided her over to the campfire near the snare. It looked like the boys were just finishing up breakfast. As soon as Pa saw him, he put down his coffee cup and hurried over.

The packhorse balked, seeing Pa coming at him that way. Pa walked kind of forceful, leaning into it, like there was a wind against him. Too, he was squinting right at that packhorse, his head tilted to one side, wondering.

Pa was a wide-built man, not so tall, but big at the shoulders and such. His face had a squarish shape to it, the jaws pretty sharp and wide, forehead the same, and even his front teeth sat kind of boxy in his mouth. He wore his moustache in handlebars, black like his eyebrows, though his hair had some gray up around the ears. Right now his face looked sunburned from the week's ride in the snow, and there were little beads of ice at the fringes of his moustache. "I thought we were going to have to go looking for you." He motioned toward the packhorse. "Where'd you get that thing?"

"Roki lent him to me," Rube grunted as he pried himself off that backbone.

"Roki! He up here?"

Rube nodded, finding the ground a mighty welcome place, though his feet prickled numb with cold and his bones ached to move. "He's after the same stallion I was. Beautiful thing, Pa. You've gotta see him. Blue-black with four white stockings and a long star—"

"Yeah, well, what happened to Red?"

Rube couldn't keep from wilting. "Darned stallion stole her from me. Just lays hold with his wolf teeth, jerks you out of the saddle and off he goes with her. Happened to Roki's grandson, too!"

He wasn't sure whether Pa would get mad or laugh, and he wasn't sure which one he'd prefer, since he'd probably be ribbed about this for the rest of his life. Pa turned away for a second and leaned on one thumb in a back pocket while a smirk squirmed back and forth across his lips, trying to get away as a snicker. He straightened his mouth finally and squinted back around. "You mean to say . . . he just came up and took her?"

Rube bobbed his head grimly, sadly. "But I'll get her back. You just wait. I've got to help you get these mustangs home, but Roki says I can ride with them and I swear I'll get her back. And him too."

"You mean the stallion?"

"Sure."

That made Pa grin and toe the dirt some. "Son, if Roki's been chasing him all the way from the Cloud Cascades, you can bet he's next to caught by now."

"Oh no. Roki's not even trying to catch him."

"What?"

Rube shrugged. "He says he's a spirit horse, the Wind-That-Gallops. He swears they just chase him for 'good medicine' and he says we're welcome to catch him, if we can. But he says we won't."

"Spirit horse." Pa wondered, then tilted his head over the other way and shook it. "Aw, I can't—He must've been funning you!"

"No, sir. He wouldn't fun me about something like that. Not in front of the medicine man!"

"Medicine man!"

"Yeah, even the medicine man comes along. I mean it, Pa. This one's special!" He looked to the men who were saddling up and saw that they were just about ready. "So let's run these horses home so I can get back to Roki. It might take me a couple of days to find him."

"Hold on, hold on," Pa said. "Now you know I trust you and all, but if I ever have to go home without you—"

"But I'll be with Roki!"

"Oh, I know, but you'll be gone so long and you know how your mother is—"

"But, Pa, if I don't get Red quick, she might go mustang on me. That happened to Kehoni. He had his mare for four years, but she was only gone two days and wouldn't come when he called her. Red's got my saddle and my roll and my saddlebags and my Winchester and—"

"All right, all right." The palm of Pa's hand signaled for Rube to slow up some, while he looked away toward the boys. "Wait a minute," he muttered, and he shouldered off toward them.

Rube watched them talk for a minute, unable to tell anything from their gestures. His stomach rumbled, but he was too anxious to think about eating.

Then he heard the men laugh and saw Pa striding back. He did that head-lifting nod of his. "You'd better eat something quick. Roki's never slow."

Rube blinked. "Well, what about the mustangs?"

Pa smiled to himself. "I'm glad I run this outfit: I'd sure hate to work for it. Naw, see the boys are going to hold 'em here, while Jessie takes Herb down and fetches back the Johnston brothers. They can take this bunch down without us."

"Really?" He grinned.

"Come on, hurry up now. Lester's lending you his chestnut. He's a gelding."

Rube shared the joke with a smile and thought to himself then what a great Pa he had. Imagine, saving the day like that and then fixing it so he could come along, too—the expert! Red and Shadow didn't stand a chance now, and even Ma couldn't complain too much if both he and Pa were gone in the mountains too long. Now that was all right.

While Rube hurried to stuff food and gather borrowed gear, Pa kept on asking him questions about the blue-black stallion, all kinds of questions. He never mentioned Red, but he wanted to know everything Roki said about Shadow. By the time they were ready to leave, Rube was tangled up with a new piece of worry, for it was more than clear that now he had more competition than just Roki and the Indians.

Pa wanted that stallion, too, wanted him bad. He hadn't

even seen the stallion yet, but all mustangers have dreams and there's a look that grows in the corner of the eye, the same kind of look goldminers get or anybody who risks his hide in search of precious things. Yes, Pa wanted the stallion. As soon as they started off, Pa took the lead.

Chapter 4

———◆◆◆———

Rube's borrowed chestnut heaved through snow drifts in jackrabbit hops, plunging belly deep in snow each time. It was no way to chase mustangs. But snow like this was what drove Shadow and his mares down from the high roughs to where the grass was better and the ground easier to run on.

But he and Kehoni were going up now to a snow-packed crack in the bluffs where Pa figured Shadow might head for when he and Roki and the others stirred them up below. There were several ways they could go, and this was only one, maybe the worst one, but Pa said there was no use everybody chasing below when somebody might be able to head off the manada and get within roping distance of Red or Kehoni's mare, Firelight.

They found the biggest fissure in Cracked Up Canyon and headed into that maze of broken granite where the walls were close and high. The wind came hollering there, dusting off drifts and pecking their skin with sharp snow.

Rube and his chestnut puffed steam and kept going because stopping was no relief at all. He rode all hunched up within his coat and knitted scarf, tilting his head forward and to the right some so that the wind could beat his hatbrim instead of his face. His left eye squinted out to see past the flopping hatbrim, and his breath froze to a crust on the edge of his scarf.

He shivered so hard it hurt, for the fire of the chase was burning out inside him now. He was beginning to wonder if Pa and Roki hadn't sent them off on a wild goose chase. He saw not a bird, not a rabbit, not a living thing in that pass. Nothing but bright, white snow and rock walls and more of the same around every twist in the gap.

Kehoni rode behind, not passing a single word or expression, but Rube had a good idea that their thoughts were running side by side. It sounded so good when they started out, riding with Pa and Roki to get their horses back, but it didn't work that way. As soon as they all met up, Pa and Roki teamed up like old times and sent Rube and Kehoni to chase a longshot in this, the highest and most difficult pass to the Winding Stairs.

Rube had plenty of miserable moments to mull that over before he found a place where the walls widened enough to let the snow be carved down to a depth of only a foot or so. Rube stopped there and looked back, but Kehoni rode up with his head shaking. "This place's way too small!" Kehoni warned. "Wild horses could kill us here."

Rube squinted around and nodded, but before he could say anything, Kehoni's lost mare bolted from a side crack in the chasm. She just appeared that way, all of a sudden, and she did a kind of stiff-legged halt when she saw them.

Red was right behind, still saddled and carrying his gear.

Both horses balked, surprised, and they couldn't get back into that side crack because other mares were jostling from behind. More mares popped out of that crack, one, two, three.

"Here, Red!" Rube yelled, yanking down his scarf. Kehoni was calling to Firelight in Cheval, too, but Firelight dodged into the exit passage and Red went after her.

Rube and Kehoni put heels to their horses then, dashing in among the startled mares that were still coming out of the crack. They scattered, scared to see mustangers right on top of them like that. They flushed out of the way as Rube plunged into the passage right behind Red.

So it was Firelight leading down that narrow slot, with Red after her and Rube behind Red. Kehoni followed close behind.

Shadow must be back there someplace, Rube thought. He'd be the last one, bringing up the drag to make sure no mares were left behind. Rube counted himself lucky that he wouldn't have to tangle with Shadow in a place so tiny.

"Red, here Red, it's me!" he yelled. The snow came deep again, and the wind howled so loud that he was rasping his throat just to out-yell it, but he kept on calling her, sure that she'd stop if she wasn't so spooked.

He was ashamed to admit it, even to himself, but Red heard him all right. She heard him calling her and she knew who it was. When they hit the drifts, his chestnut was bounding into her tracks almost as she bounded out. But would she stop? Why, no. He yelled his throat raw in that wind, punished that chestnut something awful to hang close with her, while he called her again and again, at first with confidence as if he knew she'd stop, then with firmness, then soft again like old times. And finally he was pleading and begging for her to stop, just near to crying.

He readied his lariat, but he had a hard time twirling for the closeness of those walls. They'd widen out some and he'd try it, but then his loop would rap against stone and spoil it all, and he'd pass two better places before he could get it up and whirling again.

Finally, he threw it—and missed—got it going again, and suddenly they broke out of the crack. Beyond lay a steep trail down, a place where he'd never stop her, if he snagged her too late, so he had to try quick or not at all. His lariat whooshed overhead. He threw, and she ducked her head to avoid it. The loop raked her neck, caught her saddlehorn, and before Rube could do anything, his chestnut jarred to a halt to take up the slack.

Rube cringed, not knowing which saddle would bust first. Red tried a last bound like a fish on a line, and when the rope went taut, it caught her in a midflight. She made an "oofing" groan that he'd never heard from a horse before, and that saddle peeled right off her back, breaking the cinch with a snap he could hear.

So there she went, free of her burden at last, and his saddle and all the stuff tied to it rolled in the snow at her heels. Kehoni sped past him then, his loop swinging, his heels kicking wide, as he angled his pony down the slope after Red and Firelight.

Rube yanked hard on his lariat to see if it would come loose easy, but that tumbled saddle had wrapped it up. And all the while that crack emptied out, wild horses running all around him. He gritted his teeth and yanked rope, saw that he wasn't going to have a chance—and then Shadow appeared.

Last one out of the crack, the big black did that same

stiff-legged stop when he saw Rube. Shadow threw up his head, and Rube swallowed, fearing trouble, for they weren't but ten yards apart and Rube was blocking his way.

Yet the stallion could see that Rube's rope was all tangled up in Red's saddle and that his mares were getting away just fine. Rube tried to show in every wordless way just how helpless he was at that moment.

Neck arched and nostrils flaring, Shadow wagged his long mane and pranced a second. Then suddenly he dipped his head in a kind of salute and went on by, just flowed on by, a black liquid thing that graced the snow, bounding down the mountainside with steam at his nostrils and sunlight shining on his hair.

The chestnut under him edged to go, but Rube watched the stallion run, saw Kehoni try and fail to catch his Firelight, and he knew it was over for another time. The sultan led away his harem to the safety of the Winding Stairs.

Rube looked to the saddle, to the Winchester and all the gear still tied on, and he tried to feel relieved that at least he'd got this much back. But the loan wasn't paid, by golly. Shadow still owed him, and he meant to collect.

Pa and Roki and the rest of the Indians came out of the pass and joined him there on the lip of that valley. Pa gave him a nod when they panted up, but nobody said anything until every eye had followed that stallion out of sight. Pa grinned, rocking his head in appreciation. "He's sure all you said!"

Rube sighed as he creaked down out of the saddle into knee-deep snow. "Wish I could've gotten Red."

"That's all right," Pa said. "We'll get you another."

"Another! Why, I'm still going to catch Red!"

Roki gave him that amused smile, and Pa lifted one shoulder in a shrug. "Maybe."

"No maybe to it," he grumbled, wading snow over to where the saddle lay. He could feel that smile still going around, but he was too tired and disgusted, and most of all determined, to let them shame him into being down-hearted about his chances. "I know it won't be easy, but I aim to try extra hard."

"All right." Pa smiled. "Maybe he'll come down again next winter."

"Why, I can't wait till then!" He hefted the saddle and started back to Pa.

"You'll have too."

When Rube handed up the saddle for him to hold, their eyes met. "You—you don't mean that, do you?"

Pa worked that shoulder in a shrug again, and he tried to soften his expression. "Well, Rube, we can't chase mustangs in the Winding Stairs. Just look at 'em!"

Rube looked, though he waded back to his chestnut with his head down some. From this high pass, the Winding Stairs loomed all around, great massive peaks, white with snow against a sapphire sky. Rugged ground for mustanging, he had to allow, but to him it looked like treasure country.

"No outfit could do any good up there," Pa said.

Rube climbed up on the chestnut, marveling to himself that old mustangers like Pa and Roki could be so reluctant to chase a prize like Shadow no matter where the trail led. He never thought he'd see the day. Squinting in the brightness, he gave those mountains a long, slow look. "Well, if we throw together with Roki's Indians, we'd have twice the outfit."

Roki shook his head and held up four fingers. "Four

outfits would do no good," he said, then gestured on. "That's the land of the eagle and the mountain sheep. The peaks are not so high as some, but his stronghold is—sure, safe. He was born there and he is chief there. He knows it well and we don't."

Rube reined over close to Pa to pick up the saddle. Pa was busy taking off the bedroll and saddlebags and rifle scabbard so that Rube wouldn't have so much to wrestle on that chestnut. He sure aimed to prove them wrong, but he reckoned there was no use bragging about it in advance because he sure didn't have much to show for all his sweat so far.

"Besides, son, you've gotta remember that we're in business. It just wouldn't pay to waste our time over yonder. Why, it'd be cheaper for me to *buy* you another horse than waste a summer in the Winding Stairs."

Rube didn't know what to say. He pulled the saddle over and got it around behind him so that he was wearing it on his own back. Its weight rested on the chestnut's saddle that way and left him both hands free and the ability to bend over forwards, a funny-looking arrangement, but the most comfortable over distance. "Seems to me," he muttered, "wild horses have to run the same ground we do, good or bad."

"Sure, but with nobody riding them, they can run it better!"

"I sure want to try," Rube said softly.

Pa shook his head. "Oh no, I can see what's coming. You could waste the rest of your days up there and cost us a lot of money and worry your mother sick, and if you ever did get a rope on that stallion, why, he'd only kill you! I know that and your mother knows that, and there's the rub. Now I'll get you another horse like I said, and someday we'll go—go elk hunting over there, but don't you go pining to chase mustangs in the Winding Stairs, or we'll never have any peace at home, hear?"

Rube wilted back, astonished. That sure didn't sound like Pa talking! In fact, it sounded just like Mom was moving his lips for him. It was Mom he had to convince. Surely Pa wouldn't mind his chasing mustangs any place, at least part-time, but he knew what Mom would say, and that was plenty. Mom was real good with figures and kept all the books for the ranch. She was bound to hold that chasing Shadow and Red was way too expensive and risky for the tiny chance of success. But somehow he had to convince her he must try.

Chapter 5

————◆◆————

Mom didn't want to hear about it or even think about the Wind-That-Gallops. She had a whole list of chores for Pa and a list for Rube, and one for the hands, and another list for Uncle Ned, Pa's older brother. Only the horses and the family watchdog were going to get any rest before suppertime.

"Your mom wants to know when you'll have those chickens ready," Uncle Ned called out, as he hobbled into the backyard on his homemade crutches. Ned was near sixty and he had only one leg, having lost the other one in the Civil War. He was the local tack expert, so right now he was carrying Joe Simpson's broken girth.

"Last one." Rube sniffed. He scrunched up his nose, trying to find a way to move some fluff that drifted into his face. His hands were covered with sticky feathers, white chicken feathers, blowing fluff that itched his nose and danced away to get lost in the snow.

Their black and white mongrel named Dog quit drooling at the chickens and went to bite on Ned's crutch for a minute. They called him Dog because he was the only one within five or six miles and that was all the name he needed.

"Hey, quit that!" Ned tugged on the crutch. "Quit now. You chewed one up already. Leave me a piece of this one!"

Rube whistled. "Here, Dog!" And he tossed a handful of feathers. Dog let go then and went to chase the blowing down. "Has Pa gotten those mustangs to eat yet?"

"Not yet." Ned shuffled around to be more upwind of the blowing feathers, and started working again on the girth. He was folding new cords over the ring, then doubling the cords back and braiding them into one another. When he spoke again, he sounded more serious. "I had that talk with your pa."

Rube looked up, hopeful. "Yeah?"

Ned shifted his crutch and rocked his head regretfully. "I tried, but your pa is holding on to something he might lose any time now. He's holding onto mustanging the only way he can—by making it pay. It's rough on your mom, too, having all those extra men to feed all the time. She figures ranching takes fewer men."

"It does." Rube sighed. He found himself staring at the extra chickens there on the snow. He thought about the extra potatoes his mom was peeling, the extra coffee, extra water, extra everything. Having a bunkhouse full of mustangers meant a lot more work for her and for everybody. He shook his head. "Ranching! Everybody talks like we don't do any ranching at all now, but we do. We do! We—we raise all the horses we can, but, well, it takes two and more years to raise a full-grown horse, and just two or three weeks to catch 'em wild! Mustangs come full grown. That's why it still pays, even with the extra men."

"For the time being," Ned allowed. "But how long can that last? Most of the nags we ship out now go to harness, cheap draft ponies to pull wagons and ore carts and plows and such. They're not real good for that, either. They're just cheap!"

"I know . . . golly, how I know." He gathered up the chickens by their feet. "Thanks for trying, but—well, by the time I'm as old as Pa, Shadow will be dead of old age. He'll go to waste if nobody catches him."

Ned gave him all his sympathy in a single shrug, and Rube trudged off toward the back door. He was tired and dream-weary, almost ready now to count himself lucky for being able to do any mustanging at all.

He stamped snow off his boots on the squared logs that formed the back steps and went inside. The sudden heat of the kitchen made his face feel flushed.

Mom looked up from her potato peeling and searched his face quickly. She wore a hard kind of expression now, ready for trouble. "You still sulking?"

"Nope." He laid the chickens on her cutting board.

She gave him another quick glance, as if to see if that was so. She had small, roundish features, a face splotched with freckles, and wore little, round gold-rimmed glasses. "Feed the chickens yet?"

"Yes'm. What's next?"

"I'll need some more water."

Rube took the bucket from the end of her work table and went out again. Dog bounded up and joined him as he trod the path that curved between the outhouse and the bunkhouse, leading back to the bluff behind the ranch buildings. Both the saddlehorse corral and the mustang corral farther over were built up against that cliff, which saved a lot of fencing and allowed the spring-fed stream that ran along the base of the cliff to water horses in both corrals. The springhouse was also built up against the cliff, a tiny log hut with water gurgling out from under one corner.

All along the bluish-gray cliff, oozing springwater had dipped and frozen into layers upon layers of icicle curtains, great clusters of crystal spikes that reached down and folded over the roof, almost covering the entrance with white ice drapery.

From the path, he could hear the hack knives working in the barn over to the left. Pa and the other men were making some of their "mustang recipe" to feed the wild horses that huddled in their seven-foot-high corral.

Those mustangs had been living off buck bush and tree bark, off twigs and roots and weed stems, anything but what tame horses eat, and sooner or later they'd have to switch to eating grain. But that would take some doing, for those horses had never even seen grain. They wouldn't know what it was, and even if they did recognize it as food, their stomachs couldn't handle much of such rich food.

The mustangs were half-starved before the chase began, and after running from grain-fed horses for days with no chance to stop and eat any decent food, they were ready to drop from hunger. So Pa and the men were chopping up hay real fine and mixing it with a sprinkling of oats to start them getting used to grain.

Rube glanced to the far corral and hoped that this new bunch would eat with no problem. Sometimes they refused even to the point of starvation. If that happened, the boys would have to strap leather feedbags onto their heads, bags that held the mustang recipe right up to their muzzles all the time. That usually worked. If nothing else, the mustangs would find themselves chewing their new feed out of absent-minded nervousness.

Rube forced the heavy springhouse door to give inwards and shouldered inside far enough to dip the bucket. Ice had formed at the edges of the hole-in-the-rock pool inside, but the center was clear, so he lowered the bucket sideways and filled it slowly. Dog tried to squeeze in, of course; one of his favorite tricks was to jump into the spring, even in this weather.

"Get back. Get away now."

Rube backed out of the narrow opening and pulled shut the door. He held the bucket well away from him so as not to spill any on himself. Yet as he went, he couldn't resist the temptation to look over west toward those snowy peaks that jutted into the evening sky. The sun's last glow still lit the horizon there, a faint glow that outlined the blue-purple mountains where Shadow and Red and the others ran loose.

He paused a second to watch the deepening shades of blue that darkened the sky and brought out the stars. His mountains were fading. In a moment he wouldn't be able to see them at all.

But next morning those Winding Stair peaks would be out there just as before, just as grand, just as unreachable. They'd be waiting for him to wake up.

Yet he promised that he wouldn't sulk. So tomorrow he'd feed the horses and chickens and the pigs and their dog; he'd clean and carry and mend and do; he'd have a hundred little things to keep him busy, and all the while those Winding Stair mountains would be standing over there to remind him of Shadow.

He'd never minded ranch chores so much, but if this was going to be all, if he was going to be teased by those mountains every day—well, he wondered if he could ever look west again without feeling this ache. He wondered if it would always hurt to look at the Winding Stairs.

Chapter 6

———◆◆◆———

Sudden whinnies and Dog's barking jarred Rube awake. His eyes flinched open and he sat straight up in bed, pausing only long enough to make sure that he wasn't dreaming. But the whinnies were even louder now, lots of them, and he threw back the quilts.

"Pa!" he shouted, fumbling at his boots. "Pa, something's at the horses!"

Maybe it was a mountain lion or a timber wolf.

He could hear Pa stirring in the other bedroom. Rube didn't take time to put on pants or shirt. He just grabbed his Winchester from where it stood in the corner and pulled on his jacket as he dashed for the back door. Pa was close behind him.

They ran out into the moonlit snow and dashed toward the nearest corral. The wind clawed right through Rube's long-handled underwear, but he was too startled to care, for with every step he could hear the crash and the splintering of wood and whinnies going away in the night.

"Careful!" Pa yelled behind him. "It might be a bear!"

The bunkhouse door flapped open, men stumbling out

in long-handled underwear and boots. Rube raced them to the saddlehorse corral nearby, but as he ran he thought he could see the plank gate wrenched inwards. The corral was empty, all their saddlehorses gone!

So he ran along the high rail fence, down toward the far corral. The noise swept in that direction, more whinnies and crashing sounds. But when he got there, the gate was flat on the ground, the mustangs already fleeing. Rube threw up his arms, waved the Winchester and shouted, trying to frighten back the ones that still remained inside, but the mustangs were in a panic and they kept on coming, frantic to escape. They knocked the rifle from his hand, jostled him out of the way.

"Whoa, there!" he yelled. "Whoa!"

Yet the last horse out of the corral didn't shy. He loomed big and black, his white star flashing in the bright moonlight. It was Shadow, wild Shadow, chasing out those horses. Rube flinched back to stay out from under his hooves, choked to yell again, as the stallion plunged on by.

Pa and the other men were catching up now, the night full of shouts and running feet, but it was too late. Both corrals were empty, and there was nothing they could do but watch the stallion go flying away in the darkness. His black shape stood out against the glowing snow, his white stockings invisible so that he seemed to float as he ran, sailing off over the snow. All the whinnies grew fainter now, and within a few heartbeats they were gone.

"Was that him?" Bo Sloan shouted. "Was that the stallion?"

Rube exhaled a frosty sigh and turned around. His pa was close behind him, looking stunned, as the other men gathered in. They all looked mighty odd tromping up in long underwear and boots. Herb Fincher came up last, unable to get into the jacket he carried because his arm was in a sling.

"What'd we lose?" Herb called out.

Pa only groaned, letting his rifle barrel swing down toward the snow.

"Everything," Will muttered. "Every last one."

Herb stumbled to the battered gate, turned around and around there, as if he expected to find the horses hiding someplace. Disbelief made his face go pale. "Of all the—!" He threw down his jacket, flinging it hard against the snow. Here he'd broken an arm catching those mustangs, and now they were gone. "All those—!" His voice trailed away into helpless panting.

"And the remuda, too," Will said. There was a hint of appreciation in his voice. "He sure fixed it so we can't go after him quick."

Pa glared at Will sideways, unable to share his appreciation. "The saddlehorses will be back," he told them firmly. "They can't be any more scattered than the ones we run loose on the range anyway. Come sunup, we'll take some feed and go coax a few into bridles, that's all."

"All except my mare," Gibb Russell muttered. "I'll bet he added her to his collection. Danged horse thief!"

Rube stood by, silent, his hands working to button up the jacket he wore. He was staring at the gate, at the way it was kicked inward, at the way the hinges stood twisted. No other mustang had ever been able to kick that gate open, but then again, no other mustang ever tried it from the outside. Their gates were built to keep wild horses in, not out, and from this direction the hinges couldn't hold.

That much was easy to understand. Yet what was Shadow doing down here, when only two days ago he was fleeing into the Winding Stairs with Roki and the others after him? Maybe the snows up there brought them all down again. Maybe Roki was in the foothills now, wondering where Shadow went.

Rube turned to his pa. "Do you suppose that Red might've led him here?"

"I don't know." Pa shivered. "I don't know. Let's go to bed. Everybody! We've gotta start early."

"No complaint there," somebody mumbled, and they all started to hurry off, some of them still grumbling about horse-thieving horses and about the mustangs they'd just lost.

When Rube and his pa reached the house, they found Mom standing on the back steps, waiting. She clutched a quilt around her. "Well?" she asked, when they got closer.

"Shadow!" Pa shivered. "He ran off the horses. All of 'em."

"You saw him?"

"It was him all right," Rube cut in. His teeth were beginning to chatter.

Mom opened the door ahead of them so Rube and his pa could rush inside. Even without a fire in the kitchen stove, it felt warmer inside.

"I better get some breakfast started," Mom said. There was resignation in her voice. "I reckon you'll want to start early."

Rube listened to the way she said that and he wondered. Did she really mean . . . ?

Pa tried to comfort her as she went to the stove. "Might be easier than you think. Those new mares are pretty weak, and they won't be able to eat much on the run. If we stay after them, they can't keep up. They can't."

"Poor things," Mom said. "Still, I suppose it's more important to catch that stallion." She put a bitter edge on that word, as if she didn't want to speak his name. The cast-iron skillet clattered loudly as she shoved it to one side on the stove. She was mad. "Worse than a grizzly!" she mumbled. "A grizzly might kill a horse, but he wouldn't take them all! Not all of them. Not all at once!"

Pa nodded as he dipped two pieces of kindling in coal oil to help start the fire down inside the stove. "Yeah, I've had stallions run off horses on the range before, but I never had one dare to break into a corral."

"The point is," she said, "we can't even hope to raise horses if this stallion's going to come along and steal our mares. We've got to stop him. If we don't, he'll run us broke."

Rube glanced at his pa and fought back the impulse to whoop for joy. There was a glimmer of expectation in Pa's eye, too, but they dared not share a smile in front of Mom. That would be rubbing it in.

Still, the irony made him dizzy: to think that Shadow had done what he and Pa and Uncle Ned couldn't do! In one moment Shadow had forced Mom to change her mind. Now they had to catch the Wind-That-Gallops, no matter how difficult that proved to be.

At daybreak they got ready after some of the saddle horses came back. The men gathered the remuda and loaded packhorses with supplies, and they started out. There was no good reason for believing that they'd actually catch Shadow that day or that week or that month, especially since stallions so often shied from rail traps and managed to escape even when their manadas were caught. The whole Tucker outfit rode with fresh excitement now, hopes aimed at a prize far greater than the mountains had offered in years. Even Herb Fincher begged to go along, though Pa couldn't let him, of course.

Snow made tracking easy until that afternoon, when more snow came to hide Shadow's trail. They found Roki and his Indians up in the foothills. They had been following Shadow's trail down from the Winding Stairs, and all agreed it must be a hard winter coming if the Wind-That-Gallops was determined to spend the season in the foothills.

They saw nothing on the second day, but on the third day out they picked up Shadow's trail once more. He had a huge manada with him now, and that herd left quite a track. They followed the prints north toward the Cloud Cascades, but once Shadow sighted them the speed of the chase increased.

Soon the mares Shadow had taken from the ranch began to lag behind. Shadow tried to keep them moving fast enough. He nipped and kicked at the stragglers, whinnied his demand to run, run, but his new mares were so weak from hunger that they couldn't stay up with the others.

Rube and the others began to gain on them. Since Shadow was always the last in the bunch, that put him ever closer to the men and ropes that followed. The men got a good look at the stallion Rube had raved so much about, and their shouts and whoops echoed across the snow.

Finally, as the riders drew closer, Shadow had to leave the stragglers behind and run on with the others. Joe Simpson, Gib, and the Long brothers broke away to head off the winded mares. They managed to turn them toward a box canyon, where the mares were only too glad to stop. Then four men stayed behind to guard the mares while Rube and the others rode on after Shadow.

Again the pace increased, for now Shadow was running without stragglers. He had only the mares he had brought down from the Winding Stairs, his own manada led by Firelight. Red was still with him, of course, and she gave no sign of slowing him down. After all, she'd grown up wild in these very canyons, and now that she ran as a mustang again, only her horseshoes gave any clue she'd ever worn a saddle or bridle. Rube didn't know how she got rid of that bridle—maybe Shadow chewed through a strap—but she was free of her tack now and ran like the others, swift to Shadow's every order.

They raced along ridges, valleys and gullies, down rocky slopes and up through trees. They wove through aspens and climbed through the pines, their tracks always plain in the snow.

The idea was to keep the wild ones running, never giving them time to eat or rest. They called that "walking down wild horses," but there was no walking about it. The trick was to stay after them at a steady pace until the mustangs reached the limits of their territory and circled back again. Mustangs tended to stay in one huge area, sometimes thirty miles across, always circling back when chased too far. Once the men had that territory figured out, they could set up a base camp where some of the riders could rest while others stayed after the wild ones in relays, always at a steady pace. Mustangs liked to run hard, stop to grab mouthfuls of buckbush or tree bark, then run hard again when the men caught up. But no horse could run as far that way as at a smooth and easy gallop.

Shadow had the same instincts as most: he always seemed to want to be far enough ahead that nobody could ever catch up to him. So he drove his mares hard, always looking for a place to disappear.

They came to a canyon where the granite sloped on

each side, angling steeper and steeper toward the top. Snow speckled the bluish rock, filling every crack and depression where the wind couldn't sweep it away. Low clouds stirred up there, gray clouds that hung about the mountains, hiding the very top of the canyon's rim.

Right away Shadow signaled Firelight to climb. She took the mares on up the slope, leading them diagonally up and across the high granite face on the left. Their hooves clipped on bare rock, following a crease made by the running of snowmelt in the summer—a water track, nothing more.

"Try for Red!" Roki shouted, as he charged out in front. Rube followed, the two of them leading the outfit up the slanting wall, their horses picking the same route chosen by Firelight.

Rube strained to imagine the path they'd take, never sure from second to second that there was any way down from there but *down*. All wild horses climb better than saddlehorses weighted down with riders: even their hooves are harder and tougher, especially adapted for running in the rocks. Yet even among wild ones, there are some with a special courage for racing on walls. Rube remembered what Roki had said the other night about Shadow's being able to run where nobody could ride.

Rube was riding one of Pa's old favorites, a gelding bay named Crazy. His iron horseshoes clattered and slipped on the rock, but he kept on trying. The angle got steeper and steeper, the footing less sure with every lurching bound, but Crazy wouldn't stop. That was how he had got his name.

Red had the same slippery problem, though she didn't have any weight on her back to make it worse. The iron on her forefeet struck sparks as she chopped at the rock, and it looked as if she'd already lost one of the shoes off a hind hoof. Mares bunched up behind her, slowed down by her slipping, so when she found a wide place, she hugged the mountain and let them squeeze by.

Roki hooted to see her stopping, but Shadow wouldn't pass and leave her. The stallion shook his head, insisting that she try. She looked back at Roki and Rube, and for an instant Rube thought he might have her again. But she turned and lunged again at the narrow track, this time losing the other back shoe. The worn-out iron skipped away like a stone and fell clanking down the mountainside.

That gave her better traction behind, where most of the weight and the climbing work fell. Her bare hooves gripped the rock better, allowed her powerful haunches to throw her up and up. Then another shoe spun loose, on her right forefoot this time. It hung loose by one nail for another lunge, then popped loose and slid away.

Now she had only one left. When that was gone, her hooves would either fail or work much better. Either they'd split from nails wrenching loose, or the special toughness of her mustang's hooves would give her the footing of a mountain goat.

Roki's unshod pony still gained. But when they reached the dipping wide place where Red had stopped, Rube had to give it up. "Whoa, whoa, easy!"

Shadow and Red and the other wild ones bounded up an even steeper grade. They moved like smoke upon the rock, like a flight of cliff swallows sailing at the sky. Then Firelight reached the clouds that moved about the canyon rim, and one by one, the mustangs faded away into the clouds.

Roki never got near them. Just a few yards ahead, his

pony lost all footing and fell hard on its left side. Roki jumped from the saddle as his pony went down, jumped to the left where the mountain leaned close to his shoulder. He grabbed the rock when he hit, and clung there to keep from falling onto his struggling horse.

The pony lay on the path itself, his legs splayed out over the edge, hooves trying to find a hold somewhere. Roki spoke to him quickly in Cheval and threw down the reins.

"I hope we haven't killed these horses!" Rube hollered at him.

"There was no place to stop," Roki said. "Only places to fall down."

"Yeah, well, they're all still there. Look, if your horse can back down here, I think we can turn around."

"Good, but get off your horse. Let them go down by themselves."

Rube dismounted and watched anxiously as the old man's pony trembled to stand. The pony's legs quivered, his white-rimmed eyes revolving in their sockets, staring at the distance below. Roki made small noises of encouragement and spoke to him in Cheval. Then Roki lowered himself to the path and took the bridle by the bit, urging the pony to inch backward down the slanted ledge. That took some doing, for horses hate to back down anything steep. His hooves moved jerkily on the trodden snow.

Rube didn't want to be blocking the way if that pony came down too fast, so he hurried to make Crazy turn around at the widest place. The spot was just big enough. Once he had the gelding turned, he let him go on down on his own. Crazy kept his forelegs stiff, squatting back on his haunches. When his forefeet began to slide, the gelding put his rear right down on the rock, using his rump as a drag anchor. Rube followed, his fingers searching out handholds on the rock, his slick cowboy boots unsteady.

He could see his pa waiting for him at the bottom and he wished Pa hadn't seen that ride.

When they came down, Pa said, "Well, at least we got back the horses he took."

"But Mom said it's more important to catch Shadow. Suppose he comes back and takes them again?"

"Yeah, but I can't stay up here all winter. I'll have to go back and help the boys get those mustangs home, then repair the gates, make them stronger—"

"But we've still got feed for the horses and jerky for us. If we stay after him, some day he's got to wear down, or just make a mistake or something."

"Let's see what Roki says." Pa raised up in the stirrups and called out to him, "Roki, do you want to stay after that bunch?"

Roki nodded quickly and motioned toward Rube. "If we can have your son with us. He has much courage."

Pa flicked an uncomfortable glance toward Rube and resettled himself in the saddle. "Let me think about that . . ."

Roki made an agreeable gesture and went over to where Hand-in-the-Fire was searching out some jerky.

"We could split up," Rube said. "If I stayed with Roki, we could keep Shadow busy, and you could go on back. Who knows? We might catch Red, or—"

"Couldn't Roki do that without you?"

"Well, sure, but couldn't you do without me? I'd rather stay after Shadow and Red."

"Yeah, I know."

Rube waited, afraid to say more.

Pa looked back to see that Roki was far enough away, then he leaned closer. His voice went to a whisper. "Look, Roki goes at this kind of hard. He's a good man, but, well, when he's after a mustang—What I'm trying to say is it's not safe to follow Roki too close sometimes."

"I'll come home in one piece. Honest, Pa."

"Just see that you do." Pa straightened up. "Your mother won't like me leaving you here like this. But I'm sure that's what you want and you've got to grow up some time."

Pa began calling the men together, getting ready to go back. Rube smiled after him, proud and pleased to be trusted this way, as he wrapped his scarf higher to shield his face from the blowing cold. The dark sky above was beginning to throw sleet.

Chapter 7

———◆———

Rube chased the stallion on and off all winter, never with any luck. Shadow and his manada ranged north and south along the foothills of the Winding Stairs, an area that Red knew very well. She knew all the best places to build mustang traps, all the places to avoid. Farther north toward the Cloud Cascades, Firelight knew the ground. She and Red seemed to take turns leading the manada, depending on which mare knew the area better. It was an odd arrangement, quite rare among jealous leaders, but it made their territory twice as large and made it twice as hard to work them in relays.

In the spring, when the snows melted and the mares had their new colts, Shadow led them to safety in the Winding Stairs. Rube and the others had to wait until those colts were old enough to eat grass before starting after them again, for new colts would always be the slowest, the first to fall behind in any chase, and catching an unweaned colt would mean killing it, nothing more. There would be no way to feed them fresh milk in the mountains and keep them from starving.

Later in the spring he rode with Roki, and then with a bunch of professional mustangers who came up from Colorado. Word was getting around about Shadow and his mountain fortress.

There was plenty of game of all kinds, but most of the smaller game took too much time to gather and didn't go far enough among a crew of hungry men. Mostly they lived off deer and elk, for even a small elk gave them hundreds of pounds of meat. They kept it fresh by tucking it in a hole dug in a glacier, but eventually a grizzly found the meat and dragged it away.

Streams ran swift with snowmelt, meadows colored up with wildflowers. Sometimes, down by the streams, the smell of wild mint overpowered the other green smells of pine and spruce and alpine fir. Everywhere Rube looked the beauty was awesome, even though he had to share it with mosquitoes and biting green flies.

By summer more mustangers arrived—outfits from Nevada and New Mexico, Arizona, and West Texas. Not many were still professionals; most were retired, oldtimers who longed for one more chase, one more glimpse of a truly fine wild stallion. They came at different times, but three of the outfits stayed long enough to band together, making the largest group of mustangers ever to ride the Winding Stairs.

They had little luck. Even though skilled and experienced, the men weren't used to the high mountains and thin air. Both men and horses found themselves gasping for breath. Most were accustomed to hunting wild horses in desert areas, the unwanted ranges where water was scarce. There, men chased mustangs from watering to watering, and even though wild horses could go for five days without drinking, a big outfit could guard all the water for miles around.

Yet the Winding Stair was a fountain of crystal water. Springs poured from the rocks, every low place had its brook, and some of the greenest-looking meadows were actually bogs where the mud thawed to a depth of almost two feet in summer. Even by early fall, patches of snow still lay among the shadows of rocks and large trees.

It was a far different land, and it was Shadow's land. The canyons and valleys twisted and wove one through another, some doubling back on themselves, some leading through areas where boulders as big as houses studded the land. They offered hiding places and a thousand little paths for escape. And always there were the slopes, angled plates of rock where ice and granite made it hard for horses to carry riders. Shadow always seemed to know a place where his mares could climb away out of reach.

Some of the men were hurt; one died. A young man named Bratcher from Arizona tried to cross a big patch of icy snow on one of the mountains. The patch looked almost level, but slanted gently away toward rocks. Rube hollered to stop him, for the sun melt and the night freeze had turned the slant to glaze. Young Bratcher's horse fell down at the edge of it and started to slip slowly on the angled ice. At first horse and rider slid so slowly that Bratcher was laughing, trying to get to his feet. But the farther they went, the faster. Their scrambling only made them pick up speed, faster and faster down the slick, until suddenly the ice ended and rider and horse were dashed to death on the rocks.

The oldtimers tried all their usual tricks. They set up a camp so that most of the riders could rest or build rail traps while others rode on after Shadow. It was a system that worked in the foothills, but here Shadow led the men so deep into his maze that their relays had trouble finding one another. He had a world to himself in the Winding Stairs, where he and his mares could disappear for days at a time.

By fall, most of the visiting mustangers went home, and Roki's Chevals showed up for another try. Rube sent a message home that he was all right and went on with the Indians once more.

They stayed on until late October, but even the Indians couldn't lead him any closer to Shadow. Tracking was difficult because other bands of wild horses roamed the Winding Stairs, and their hoofprints looked much alike. Even when they had Shadow in sight, there was no way to prevent him from climbing the rocky slopes. They could never make him go one way or another. All they could do was follow him as far as they could.

"Do you believe me now?" Roki said. "He is a gust of wind that wears a horse's skin. He is a mountain spirit, a thing of magic."

Rube never knew what to make of the old man's spirit talk, except to notice that Roki never joshed him so much when Pa was around. He wished that Pa could be with them now. Then one day, as Rube rode his winded gelding back toward camp, Hand-in-the-Fire brought word that Pa had come up with two men and a pack mule loaded with coffee and oats and other such things. Rube hurried to camp, eager to see Pa.

When he got there, he found Roki and two other Indians and Joe Simpson, and Russian Will gathered around

Pa, who was lying against his saddle, soaking wet, obviously in pain.

"What happened?" Rube hollered, jumping down from his horse.

Pa set his teeth against each other, eyes squinting. "Of all the—! I always figured I'd fly to glory from the back of some mustang, but—no! I slip on a wet rock and go down with a coffee pot in my hand!"

Rube looked to Roki, who was studying Pa's right leg. The old man shook his head sadly. "It's broken. Not so bad as some, but broken, yes."

"I know that!" Pa winced. "I heard it go!"

Rube suddenly felt chilled. "Who's going to set it?"

"No use," said Roki. "Not here. No matter how tight we splint it, the bones would only come apart when you travel."

"All right. We'll take him home first, but we better start right now."

It was agreed that Joe and Will would ride ahead to fetch the doctor and have him at the ranch when Pa arrived.

They made a splint by lashing two strong branches along Pa's leg. Roki used elk rawhide to bind it up tight. Then they made one of those drag litters that the French trappers called a *travois* by tying two long poles to the saddle on Pa's horse, with the ends of the poles dragging the ground. A lacework of rawhide kept the poles from spreading apart and made a basketlike pouch for the hides and blankets that formed his stretcher. It was a fairly comfortable place to lie, as long as the horse stood still, but once the horse started off, the poles bumped and grated. It was a jarring, jolting way to go, so rough that they had to tie him to the stretcher to keep him from slipping off, but it was the only way to carry him.

Rube tried to pick the smoothest way and think of nothing but getting Pa home. But all the way the thought nagged him that now he'd have to take his father's place and responsibilities. He'd have to stay home and run the ranch. If he caught any mustangs at all, it would have to be in the foothills close to home.

Chapter 8

❖❖❖

"Watch that pinto, Will!" Rube shouted, as he waved his lariat and reined his horse to keep the wild ones racing together.

It was April now, the end of a hard-luck winter. Heavy snows had kept him from mustanging and Pa's leg didn't mend right. Somehow it started to mend crooked, so Doc had to break it all over, then reset the bones again. It seemed to be knitting straight now, but Pa was still laid up and Rube missed his company.

Nine mares and yearling colts splashed across the swollen brook, breaking the icy crust that still clung at its edges. The other men hooted and waved jackets and ropes, crowding the mustangs, forcing them onto the meadow that stretched toward home.

That meadow narrowed up ahead. Low bluffs crowded in to make a natural funnel that led toward the corral. A long wing of sturdy fence reached out to keep any mustangs from spilling around and escaping beyond. The fence angled toward the gate of the mustang corral, which stood open now, awaiting the harvest from the foothills.

When the mustangs saw all those buildings and fences ahead, they tried to balk. The men shouted and whistled even louder and waved their jackets to keep them spooked. The lead mare tried to break away, but other mustangs followed so closely that the herd didn't break up; it only shifted direction, this way and that, as the herding instinct kept them running together.

Joe Simpson, riding point, headed straight for the open gate, hoping the lead mare would follow him inside. Joe galloped his horse inside and Russian Will followed him. The mares took their lead, and suddenly all of the mustangs were jostling to squeeze through the gate, as if that gate was the only way to safety and not a trap. The last two had to wait a split second, and in their panic that was too long. They broke away, a white mare with a glass eye and a pinto with an odd neck.

"Let 'em go!" somebody yelled, but letting the scrubs go free to multiply was what ruined much of the mustang breed. Now they needed every head, regardless, so Rube reined out and kicked after them.

While the white mare dodged between the smokehouse and the well, Rube went after the pinto. His circling loop cut the air overhead, then he threw. As soon as he saw the loop necktie, he reined back with his left hand, the hand that held the coil, while his right hand grabbed rope and made a fast dally around the saddlehorn. When the rope went straight, the mare's head jerked hard to the side. She stumbled, nearly fell, but regained her footing and fought to escape.

"Get out!" he heard Mom yelling. "Get out! Out!" And looking away a second, he saw the other mare fleeing from between the smokehouse and the outhouse, Mom after her with a broom.

Rube started to grin, but felt his rope angle sideways and suddenly he realized that he shouldn't have looked away. Old Crazy was a marvel at the chase, but he was no great talent as roping horse. He didn't have the rope sense to guard an animal all by himself, the way a true roping horse ought to. Rube tried to yank him around so that the taut rope was out in front of the saddle again, but it was too late. The mustang was already swinging around, and her sideways jerk on the saddle pulled old Crazy right off his feet. Rube jumped from the saddle as he went down, jumped and rolled clear.

The pinto mare caught her rope on one of the posts that held the clothesline, and she started to wrap herself up. Rube scrambled back to Crazy, freed his rope from the saddlehorn, and held on tight, as the mustang changed direction and tried to unwrap herself from the pole. The men were closing up the gate now and running to help him.

"Wa-hoo!" Herb Fincher hooted. "You got a live one there!"

"Then come and help!"

Bo Sloan was still in the saddle, so he arrived first at a gallop, his lariat swinging.

With two ropes on the pinto now, the exhausted mare began to lose fight. Herb Fincher and Joe Simpson had the other one under control, and in a few minutes they had both mustangs in the corral where they belonged.

Rube gathered up his lariat, still panting, still trembling from the long and nervous ride. His lower lip began to throb again, all puffy and sore where a mare had kicked him hours ago, but even with that, he felt good somehow. For once again he'd been able to bring back some broom-tails, a few anyway. Now he had nine more to add to the dozen he had penned already in the saddlehorse corral. That made twenty-one. And even though some of them were just weaned colts and awkward yearlings, he hoped he could get enough for them to pay the bank.

"At least we'll be able to make the mortgage payment," Mom said. "That's the important thing."

"I'll be glad when we can go to work for ourselves," Rube replied. "Seems kind of funny working for a bank."

"We're just paying back what was lent us, that's all. If we didn't have everything tied up in land and stock and harness and such—well, we might be able to do without the bank. But the only way we could have the ranch and the money to run it at the same time was by borrowing."

When Mom went inside, Rube wandered over to the corral where the men were looking over the new bunch of broomtails. It was a standard ritual, each man with a foot on one of the lower rails, elbows draped on another rail, while they peered through and jawed about what narrow-withered, glass-eyed crowbait they'd caught this time. None of the men said anything like that during the chase, of course, for wild horses have a way of looking grand when running free. It was only after they were penned that they began to look scrawny.

"They'll sell," Uncle Ned said.

"Then maybe we'll all get paid for once," Joe Simpson joked.

"Yeah," Rube muttered, "I'm real sorry about that, but it's been a strange winter, and now the bank's breathing down our necks."

"I know," Joe said. "Don't get me wrong. I'm used to waiting for back pay."

"That's right," said one of the other men.

"Well, everything's going to be better now." Rube

grasped the top of the plank gate and gave it a firm shake, thinking to himself that only Shadow could ruin this now. It had been a year since Shadow kicked down that gate, but the hoofmarks were still there on the planks to remind him. The flat strapping on the gate side of the hinges bore marks from Uncle Ned's blacksmithing.

"Don't worry." Uncle Ned grinned. "I think it'll hold."

"Think he'll come back?"

"Might." Ned shrugged. "While you fellas were gone on this latest ride he hit the Neddlestons and the Rathkeys. Ran off all the horses they had on the range, broke into a corral."

"Shadow?" Will asked.

Ned bobbed his head. "They even wanted us to go in with them on a bounty they're offering."

Rube was alarmed. "A bounty on *Shadow*—dead?"

"No way to keep 'em from offering one," Ned said.

Rube found himself studying the slide bars of the gate again. "I know this looks all right, but, golly, if we were to lose this bunch . . ."

"Yeah, we could lose the ranch," Ned added. "I was thinking about that last night."

"We all were!" Joe said. "More'n one of us has seen a ranch auctioned off by some bank, and all for the lack of a couple of loan payments. But that's the law."

Rube nodded uncomfortably as he reached up to grip the top rail on the seven-foot fence. "Let's not take any chances. Let's put all the mustangs in this corral, both bunches, then tie the gate shut. Tie it at both ends, hinge and latch. We'll put the saddlehorses over in their corral and we'll tie that gate, too. Do we have any chain?"

"Some."

"Then tie 'em with chain. I don't care how long it takes

to do or undo, I just want to make sure those horses don't get away."

The men agreed. "Beats the idea I had," Will said. "I was thinking about putting the buckboard right here, kinda like a barricade."

"Then we'll do that, too," Rube said. "That way he couldn't even get near the gate."

Combining the two bunches of mustangs was easy because there was a third gate inside that led through the seven-foot wall of logs separating the two corrals. Rube had them tie that gate shut also, just in case.

Only the gates gave him much worry, for they were made of mill-sawn planks—strong planks at that, each about an inch thick—but nothing to compare with the stout poles that formed the high fences of both corrals. Even the saddlehorses' corral had to be built extra tall and strong, for sometimes they needed it to hold mustangs.

The fenceposts were tall and sturdy and set as deep as possible in the rocky ground. No post stood alone. All were set in pairs, close together, so the ends of the rails only had to be stacked into the slot between the fenceposts. No nails or bindings were needed, for the rail ends overlapped, one on another, lacing together between the two posts.

None of the rails was split lengthwise, either, for that kind of rail had sharp edges that could injure man or horse. These were trimmed saplings, each round and straight and slender. On the outside of the fence more poles slanted up from the ground to brace the top of each pair of fenceposts.

Before Rube went to bed that night he fingered his "magic" rope, looking at the different colors of hair in the lariat. Now that Shadow had a price on his head, he wondered if he'd ever get a chance to test his rope against the stallion. Any day now somebody might tell him that Shadow was dead, killed by some idiot with a rifle.

He remembered what the shaman said about that rope more than a year ago, something about the magic of the rope being made stronger because it was plaited from hair of all the horses he had ever loved. The shaman had said Rube's own hair could make that magic stronger if plaited into the rope. Rube had a strange feeling that maybe love and power and dreams had some kind of reality of their own.

Suddenly he yanked out a few strands of his own hair. Gripping a two-inch section of the rope with both hands, he twisted and pushed to loosen the plaiting, then worked a few strands of his hair into it. He would try anything to catch the Wind-That-Gallops.

That night, as he slept, Shadow galloped through his dreams, leading him along dizzy cliffs where the clouds reached down to gather the wild ones into the sky.

But when the dog started to bark outside and the horses began to raise a commotion, his dream soured into a nightmare and he woke up shaking. He knew before he could get his boots on that Shadow was at the horses again.

As he stumbled outside, he saw the dark shape with the white stocking feet churning away into the night. He raised the Winchester to his shoulder, following the dark comet in its sights, but his finger was helpless at the trigger. Shadow was running away with all the mustangs he'd worked so hard to catch, all the mustangs he needed to pay the bank. Yet he couldn't press the trigger; he just couldn't.

Rube looked at the rifle in his hands. "Some idiot with a rifle," he muttered, wondering why he'd been so quick to bring the Winchester instead of the lariat. He had not even picked up the rope.

Numbly he ran toward the farthest corral. On his way, he passed the saddlehorse corral. The remuda there was safe, at least, the gate still tied shut. He didn't know what to expect when he got to the mustang corral. To his surprise, the buckboard still blocked the gate and the gate itself had not been broken. He climbed onto the buckboard and strained to see in the darkness. The corral was empty all right, every precious mustang gone, yet he couldn't see how they had got out.

The men were catching up now, but Rube couldn't wait for them. He climbed down into the corral and began running along its fence. He couldn't imagine how Shadow could make a hole in the fence itself, but with every step he told himself that it couldn't be magic.

At the farthest corner of the pen, where the fence crossed the tiny stream and joined the base of the cliff, he found the rails spilled on the ground. One pair of fenceposts had been kicked over, broken off at the ground somehow.

He knelt down and touched them. The posts felt hard and strong, but when he pinched the wood at ground level, he groaned. It was soft and wet, rotten from standing in wet soil beside the stream.

Shadow probably picked this spot because it was the farthest from the ranch buildings. He was probably shy of the dog and wanted to kick at a place on the fence where he wouldn't be discovered so quickly. What an irony, Rube thought, that these were also the posts nearest the water that were rotting undergound.

"Now what?" he whispered to himself.

Chapter 9

‹◆›

"I know it sounds mean," Mom said as Rube tied on his saddlebags next morning, "but it's not mean to want to keep your horses, is it?"

"Guess not," Rube muttered, his mind frozen to the moment when he had that stallion in his sights. The thought of squeezing the trigger still made his insides crawl.

"But I'm right, aren't I?" she asked gently. "It would be easier to shoot him than to catch him." She handed him his Winchester as if it were a broom, holding it by the very end of the barrel, up near the sight, and the look in her eye left no way to mistake her meaning.

Rube took the rifle and slid it into the scabbard that angled along the saddle's right side. His breath came as a sigh. If only things could be different. But no. Shadow had his own way of turning things around: when men climbed to his fortress and ran down too many of his mares, Shadow came down to the ranches and stole more to replace them. There was a strange kind of justice about that.

"The reward's a hundred dollars," Mom said, as if that might make him feel better. "That's half what we need to pay the bank—"

"Only half?"

"Well, half's more than we've got right now! It's not easy finding that much money. Everybody we know's just hanging on. Besides, half might be enough right now, if we stop that outlaw. The bank knows we can't start over with that stallion taking our horses every time."

Rube nodded. "I better get going." He grabbed his bedroll, threw it up behind the cantle, and laced it down.

"Sure you don't want more men along?"

"One's enough. I don't want a crowd."

Mom watched him with a growing sadness. "Maybe it won't count for much right now, but . . . I am proud of you."

"Well, I'm not."

"But I am. I—I know how hard this is."

He stepped up into the stirrup and swung into the saddle. Russian Will was trotting his horse over, ready to go.

"One more thing." Mom spoke reluctantly. "They'll want some proof he's dead, that it's really him and not just some black horse. Everybody knows his markings, so you'll have to skin him."

Rube's stomach wrenched. Skin him! Wasn't it bad enough having to *kill him?* He kicked old Crazy, anxious to get away.

Then he glanced back at the house and saw Pa looking out a window at him. Pa raised a hand, and Rube raised his in good-bye. Never had he seen a man look so sad as his Pa did.

They followed the trail up into the foothills. As they started the climb, they could see into the next meadow valley where the Neddleston ranch lay. Wagons and men were at work down there, a whole crew of ranch hands busy stringing fence.

"Think that'll work?" Rube asked Russian Will.

Will shrugged. "Barbed wire works all right."

"But they can't fence the world!"

"They can fence their piece of it, if they do it little at a time."

Rube shook his head. "Sure going to feel strange having a fence down there. We'll have to go around by the road."

"Better get used to it. You should see other parts of the country. Ranchers gone fence wild. Fences everyplace."

Up over Snake Ridge, then along Saddle Creek, they tracked the wild horses toward the Winding Stairs. On the way they spotted the white mare with the glass eye and the pinto with the odd neck. Apparently Shadow didn't want them in his manada. Stallions can be fussy like that.

In early afternoon the tracks disappeared.

Will got down off his horse and led the animal as he walked the ground in ever larger circles. He stooped very low as he went, sometimes squatting down to feel the soil. The black floppy hat that he had tugged down over his sagebrush almost always hid his eyes. Finally, he scratched his gray beard and motioned toward a stand of rock. "That's where he went. Up over that rock there."

"How can you tell?"

"I can smell their trail. Can't you?"

"No, and neither can you."

"Well, where would you go? The ground is softer there and there and over yonder there, so if you went any of those ways, you'd leave a trail. But since there ain't no trail, they must've gone up over those rocks."

"Let's see if we can pick it up on the other side."

They found the trail again and followed until it disappeared once more, then used the same method to find it. Each time they could look at the lay of the land and guess where horses would go, and each time their guess led them to fresh prints on softer ground beyond.

Later that afternoon they heard horses squalling with fury close ahead. It sounded like two horses fighting! Any stallion who runs with a fine, large manada meets other wild challengers bent on taking his mares.

They hurried to tie up their horses, and Rube took down his Winchester. He watched the top of the tree-covered ridge, his breath coming short and tense. Slowly he worked the rifle's lever, cocking it without much noise.

Together he and Will crept forward, climbing the slope, then crawling the last bit of the way. Anticipation made his hands sweat. Then he peeked over the rim.

In a shelflike clearing close by, Shadow and another wild stallion swirled in battle. Around and around they went, their long manes and tails spread on the wind as they fought with hooves and teeth. Shadow and the sorrel kicked at each other with powerful hind legs, then whirled to stand, to rear up high and paw with sharp hooves and lunge with open jaws.

The sorrel looked younger, less experienced, but he was strong and quick and determined to have those mares for himself. The sorrel had a barrel chest and a short neck, none of the quality of Shadow's blood, yet beauty was no advantage in a test of teeth and hooves.

Rube had seen stallions challenged before, but usually it was only a ritual fight and one stallion would give way before things got too rough. But this was different. These stallions were too well matched for one to give up quickly. Now, as the blood began to show, they fought to a killing frenzy that had to end in death for one of them. They struck and tore at each other with all their power, screamed and squalled at each other, nostrils wide. When Shadow's jaws slipped off the sorrel's hide, his teeth slammed shut with a pop so loud and so shrill that it made Rube's teeth hurt just to hear it.

Russian Will edged closer, as they lay there on the rim. He motioned toward the Winchester. "I'll do it," he whispered.

Rube bit his lower lip and watched them battle. He had made up his mind that if he got another chance he would have to shoot the Wind-That-Gallops. He'd have to do it himself, but it troubled him because it was such a close and easy shot. The drifting clouds of dust kicked up by the stallions told him that the horses were upwind, so they wouldn't pick up the human scent even this close. He had plenty of time to aim, a close and easy shot.

Yet it wasn't easy either. He'd told himself over and over that Shadow was just a pest now, a savage nuisance that needed killing for the good of the ranch. But now, as he took aim, as he looked at that beautiful black, his old fascination with the animal took hold.

"Do it now," Will whispered. "Do it now while he's busy. He'll never know what hit him." There was an anxious pause. "Want me to do it?"

Rube shook his head slowly, determined to gather the nerve. All the while his eyes searched the clearing. He saw the deep ravine that angled from the right, saw the way it cut the ground up close to the stallions, and then his spirit brightened. A crazy feeling tingled through him, and he uncocked the rifle.

"Now!" Will insisted. "Do it now!"

Rube shook his head again. A smile teased at his lips, a glimmering of hope that he never expected. "We can do that any time. Today, tomorrow, any time. From long range. But he's busy now, too busy to see me coming."

He looked to Will and saw the fear sink in—the fear and the awful temptation. That fuzzy old mustanger wanted to try it. He ached to try it, but he had the responsibility of keeping the boss's son from getting killed. His sagebrush beard swept dirt as he wagged his head so close to the ground. "No!" he breathed. "We can't!"

"Then I will."

The Russian grabbed his arm, held it tight. "Don't! He'll kill you!"

Rube pushed the rifle at him. "Then you keep me covered. But don't you shoot unless he's got me down, hear? Don't you shoot unless he's killing me." He pulled his arm free of Will's grip.

Will looked at him for a moment, a long and awful moment. He did not say yes or no. He just watched Rube edge back down the slope.

As Rube hurried to the tied horses he checked the cylinders in his .44 revolver. He shoved it back into its holster, pulled on brown leather gloves, then untied old Crazy and mounted up. He felt almost dizzy with the thought that this time—this time at last—he might get a rope on the Wind-That-Gallops.

Unlacing his coiled lariat, he shook out the loop and readied it in his right hand. As he did it, Roki's words spun through his mind: "It has the feel of magic. With such a rope, you might catch a mountain spirit."

And he thought of Roki's warning, too, about not tying his happiness to a dream. That gave him a crazy, a dangerous idea.

Taking the free end of his magic rope, he did something he'd never done before. He tied it to the saddlehorn with another slip knot. It wasn't safe that way, for sometimes it was essential to be able to let go, but he was staking everything on this moment.

"Come on," he whispered, kicking up old Crazy.

Chapter 10

———— •••• ————

Riding close under cover of the ravine, Rube hunched over low in the saddle so he couldn't be seen until the last instant. Ahead, the stallions' thudding and screaming noise grew louder. He saw the end of the ravine coming and set his teeth. His right hand cranked up his lariat, and suddenly he was on them.

"Hey-ah!" he yelled to frighten back the sorrel.

Both stallions saw him at once and nearly knocked each other down. Shadow dodged behind the sorrel, and at once the air was full of whinnies as the mares jostled to get away. Rube ignored the sorrel and mares, his eyes tied to that blue-black stallion that darted now for the shelf's edge. Shadow dipped his head, then bounded down the slope where granite had crumbled to gravel.

Rube kicked after him, his lariat stirring the sky. He didn't know if Will could cover him down there or not, or if he could stop Shadow's downhill charge, but as soon as he reached the edge and saw Shadow in the clear, he threw.

It was like a dream. The loop sailed out like a ring of smoke, and Shadow's downward race sent him right into it. The loop settled around his neck, drew smaller as Rube took a quick dally around the saddlehorn.

"Got him!" Rube grunted, teeth clenched, fists clenched.

The rope went taut with a sudden jerk. Shadow's head whipped back with the impact, his sleek muscles knotting. Old Crazy sat farther back on his haunches, trying to stop the stallion, but the crumbled granite under his hooves began to roll. His eyes went white at the edges, and he murmured. For the slope was too steep, the gravel too loose, the force of gravity too much of a help to the stallion who fought below.

Shadow put down his head and lunged. Crazy went sliding away, down and down, faster and faster, until the gelding had to give it up or be pulled over on his nose. Crazy's knees buckled first, a short hop, then his forelegs stiffened again to slide a second, then buckled again with a little jump and stiffened again. He couldn't stop, couldn't hold. All he could do was hope and slide, while the stallion dragged him down the mountain.

Shadow angled to the side, the rope sweeping after him, sweeping over small trees that clung to the mountainside. The green saplings bent and sprang back again. A dead one shattered, spraying small twigs. Then the rope caught on a rock, stretched and groaned and twanged free again. Shadow picked up speed and Crazy had to follow, now at a gallop.

Twice Rube tried to make a stand, but he only lost rope doing it. The coil of extra length he carried shrank as he had to give way again and again. He began to wish he could throw it all away, get rid of that rope! For with every passing second, he was jarring toward some bone-breaking death.

He hoped he could hold on until Russian Will could get to his horse and catch up. But he couldn't guess how long that would take, for everything was downhill for a long way ahead, and the ground got worse. There were trees down there, bigger trees and bigger rocks and a fast stream that tumbled down a crease in the mountainside. He winced at the awful distance ahead and fought to keep his gelding upright.

Shadow shifted direction, this way and that, and Crazy tried to match him turn for turn. The stallion dragged them toward the stream that churned white among the rocks. Again Rube tried to rein back, but Shadow had momentum now and Crazy had no footing that could hold. In a blink they were plunging into frigid water, hooves slipping among rocks made slick by rushing currents.

The stallion leaped to the bank again and came back, charging. Crazy shied from the hooves and fell back. He was desperate to escape the water, but as soon as he tried to climb out at a place nearby, Shadow cut him off.

The stream was full of slack rope now, and before Rube could gather it up, Shadow used his slack to dart sideways along the torrent. Crazy struggled to turn with him, to keep the rope always out in front, but he slipped and stumbled, nearly fell.

Shadow carried the rope sweeping around to the side. Rube saw it coming. "Oh, no!" But he couldn't do anything fast enough to save them. All he could do was get ready to jump.

When Shadow reached the end of the long lariat, he stood up on hind legs again with a whinny of triumph and defiance. He tossed his head when he did that, a powerful, easy-looking toss that yanked the rope so hard that Crazy went right over. The gelding made a frightened noise when he felt his hooves going out from under him. Rube swung his leg free, stepped hard on the other stirrup to push himself away. Both he and Crazy hit the water almost at the same time.

Ice water! Rube was stunned by the frigid shock. When he rolled up to gasp, his lungs felt paralyzed. For an instant all he could do was inhale in quick gasps while the water around him stung like fire.

Crazy thrashed beside him, frantic to get up, and suddenly Rube had to fight the heavy current to keep from being swept under his horse's hooves. The gelding almost got to his feet, but Shadow gave another neck-arched jerk, and again he went over on his side. Yet this time Crazy managed to twist as he fell. He twisted around so the rope went out past the front of his saddle again, and Shadow's next yank actually helped pull him to his feet.

Fast water dragged at Rube's legs, but he couldn't let Crazy run off without him. As the gelding lunged for the bank, Rube caught the saddlehorn with his left hand. Crazy's panicked struggle helped pull him out of the water.

As soon as the gelding made the bank and picked up speed, Rube stiffened his knees and bounced on his heels, trying to mount pony express style, but it didn't work. He was too exhausted and Crazy didn't have enough speed to bounce him high enough. He was all knees and elbows scrambling into the saddle, but he made it. The knotted reins were up between Crazy's ears, so Rube grabbed them back again and he was on.

Yet Crazy was thoroughly spooked now. That horse

only wanted to stay on his feet, to follow the stallion so the rope couldn't pull him down again. He and Shadow ran like frightened deer through the forest, Crazy matching him turn for turn as they wove through rocks and trees. Shadow dodged and wheeled, trying to pick a trail that Crazy couldn't follow. Then up ahead the trees thinned out and broke to a clearing where the ground was dished, but never steep, all covered with meadow grass and wildflowers.

Rube muscled up a couple of feet of slack rope. "Now, Crazy!" He reined back and let go the rope at the same time. The slack gave Crazy a chance to stiff-leg to a halt, and when the rope twanged straight again, the gelding was dug in on leveler ground.

Shadow's head yanked to the side, his whole body wheeling round until he faced Rube. His great nostrils flared as he panted, his muscles stood out as he strained stiff-legged against the horsehair rope and the saddle that squeaked under Rube.

Rube glanced to see if Will was coming, but there was no sign of him.

Then he saw the fire brighten in Shadow's eyes and the upper lip curl back to show his wolf teeth. Rube died a little, knowing what was coming. The stallion uncoiled like a rattler striking and charged, teeth open, lips drawn back, ears laid back.

Crazy shied, wheeled, and got away at a leap. Rube hung on tight while Crazy ran, then started grabbing up rope. He gathered two loops before he saw Shadow's open jaws coming just a few feet behind him.

"Back!" he cried, flaying with the coil of rope. Shadow flinched and shook his head, but did not slow. He only laid back his ears and drove for more speed.

"No!" Rube leaned away in the saddle, forward and to the left as Shadow came up steadily on his right. He tried to beat back the stallion, but his rope had no magic to stop those teeth that came for him. He pulled his right leg away from the stirrup and leaned farther to the left. Unable to take his gaze off the stallion's teeth, he did not see the pine branch that dipped low. As Crazy ran under it, the branch swatted Rube out of the saddle. He fell like someone dead, spanking the ground hard and rolling over twice. The breath dashed out of him, he lay there paralyzed while the horses thundered on.

Rube rolled over, gasping for breath, and saw the loop of rope that trailed after the horses go whisking by. It flipped pine cones off the ground, racing toward the tree where it had to stop, for the horses passed the tree on opposite sides. Crazy ran to the left, Shadow to the right. The rope between them climbed the tree trunk a way and then bit bark. The running horses pulled it tight so suddenly that it sang.

That swung the horses toward each other. They smacked together at the shoulder, hit hard, and above the thud of their bodies, Rube heard a shrill popping sound. The saddlehorn snapped off and sprang away with the rope still knotted to it. Shadow was loose!

Rube came off the ground, his numb legs hurling him at the stallion. The Wind-That-Gallops swung around to unwind the rope and pull it away from the tree. Rube dashed to the tree to stop the rope from whipping away and letting Shadow go free.

Shadow came up against a cluster of large boulders and had to shift direction to dodge them. Rube fell on the rope and caught it only twenty feet from the stallion's neck.

Then he jumped and landed with his boot heels in the ground, legs and spine rigid as a tent stake.

He couldn't hold, of course. Shadow's power made him bend his knees and hop, but he dug in again and again, his teeth grinding, his eyes squinting, his gloved fists knotted around that rope. "No you don't!"

The finest mustang in the mountains bounded only twenty feet away on his own horsehair rope. He prayed that Will would show up now, that somehow this stallion could be his.

Suddenly Shadow stopped running and whirled. He stood up on hind legs, shaking his head as he glared down, hooves threatening. There was no white in his eyes now, no hint of fear or panic; they were like angry black jewels.

Rube shrank back, the reality of this dream suddenly staring down at him. "W-Will?" he stammered, ready to run.

But then the stallion dropped to all fours, the anger in his eyes shifting slowly, changing to a kind of proud annoyance. He looked almost insulted, irritated, but very confident now that he got a good look at Rube so close and so helpless.

Rube panted and waited, both terrified and fascinated, not knowing what to think of this wild stallion that stood there and glared at him like a king being bothered by a beggar boy.

The stallion looked as if he were waiting for Rube to untie him. It was that kind of look, that proud and sure. But then Shadow glanced away up the mountain toward something that he could hear but Rube could not. And then, through the treetops, Rube thought he saw Will riding down.

Shadow looked back at Rube and stamped his feet suddenly, impatiently. Rube blinked and edged back, knowing what Shadow expected of him, but unable to pry his fingers off that rope. He had the dream in his hands now, and his fists wouldn't let go.

The stallion tucked back his chin, his neck arched, and then slowly he stepped forward, stepped toward Rube and stretched out his neck like a' goose hissing. His ears laid back when he did that, and his upper lip curled back to show the fighting teeth that were opening.

Rube stepped back, his panting growing faster. He lowered his hands along his side, his thumb searching for the reassuring steel of the .44 there in his holster. But his thumb fell on an empty holster—empty! The revolver was gone, lost somewhere!

The rope between him and Shadow fell limp as the stallion took another step forward, his head still lowered in that threatening pose, his wolf teeth shining. Rube backed away, but the stallion followed slowly. Then Shadow sprang at him.

"Will!" Rube yelled, throwing himself into a run. But he kept the rope clenched in his fists. "Will!"

Shadow snapped at his jacket on the left side, so Rube darted to the right, reached out and caught a tree with his gloved hand and swung around the trunk. Shadow lunged at him on the other side, but Rube ducked and slapped at his nose. The stallion reared back, head shaking, and Rube dodged to complete his swing around the tree.

Suddenly the stallion had a mouthful of his leather jacket. Rube peeled out of the jacket to get away, jumped over the slack rope that trailed on the ground, and then started away from the tree with rope zipping through wet gloves. Too late he realized that he should have gripped the rope and pulled it hard to snub the stallion up closer to the tree. But he couldn't take up all the slack at once, and Shadow was still after him.

Rube kept swatting at the stallion and trying to beat him away as he stumbled back along the rope. The teeth reached for him and snapped within inches of his hands. Then Shadow reached the end of his slack and the twanging rope jerked his head back, yanking his body to a halt. The stallion reared and threw himself forward again, all his weight on the rope, lunging and straining, his eyes wild and teeth snapping.

Rube had more loose rope behind him, so he crawfished all the way back to the end of it, just as Shadow wheeled and tried to kick him. Rube threw himself to the ground. He held the very end of the rope now and the broken saddlehorn. He stretched himself away the full length of his body, pressing his face in the dirt as the hooves flashed over him again and again.

"Will! Please! Will!"

The stallion stretched back and tried to stamp him with hind legs, but couldn't reach him that way. And every time the great horse kicked, his hooves arced upwards so that their upward swing cleared Rube's arms and head.

Will was coming, riding close now with the Winchester.

"No!" he cried, realizing Will would see him on the ground and shoot the stallion. "Don't shoot, Will! I've got him! I've got him!"

Yet Will rode up as if he couldn't hear over the noise of his own horse galloping.

"Don't shoot! I've got him!"

Chapter 11

◆—◆◆—◆

He had him, all right, on that horsehair rope. Even before Russian Will could lasso one of Shadow's hind legs, the phantom of the Winding Stairs was helpless on Rube's lariat. Though he kicked and fought, though he reared up screaming with wide nostrils fluttering, there was no way to stomp Rube or tear the rope apart, no way to escape at all.

Once they had him tied between two trees, one rope on his neck and the other on a hind leg, it was the end of Shadow's fight. He couldn't kick, couldn't rear, couldn't do anything but fall down if he tried. All at once he stopped trying.

Rube's teeth chattered and his muscles shook from cold and exhaustion, but he didn't care. His wildest fantasy had come true at last. Red, Firelight, and the others had got away, but their splendid stallion was his at last.

"What—what took you so long?" Rube shivered.

Will wagged his sagebrush, looking embarrassed. "Sorry. I ran for my horse so fast and so scared that—well—I scared him too! He busted a rein and run off!"

Will gave him his bedroll to help keep warm and then hurried off to fetch help while Rube settled down for the long wait. He talked to Shadow slowly and gently. He picked handfuls of green grass which Shadow wouldn't even sniff at. The stallion didn't struggle, but watched Rube with emotions that shifted from anger to interest, from anxiety to disgust, but even in defeat he never lost his dignity. He didn't fight the ropes, but stood very still, with neck arched high.

He and Rube passed long minutes just staring at each other. Shadow seemed to be studying him, alert, cautious, almost curious.

It was surprising, Rube thought, how readily he realized there was no use fighting the ropes. Most wild stallions would have wound themselves up in knots and fallen down sixty times, but Shadow was too wise for that. He obviously hated being tied, yet he stood there with quiet dignity, waiting. Waiting for what?

Worry overtook Rube's joy. What if Shadow wouldn't eat? What if he refused to be touched? Mustang stallions were noted for always making trouble unless they were gelded early. And this was a full-grown lord of the wild, the kind that rarely surrendered to captivity.

"I'll be good to you," Rube told him softly. "You'll see. We'll take it as slow as you like. We'll get those stickers out of your tail and clean that spattered mud off you, brush you down. You'll like that. You're proud enough to like that."

Eventually, Crazy wandered back to see what was going on, and Rube was glad to have the extra jerky and bedroll that were on his saddle. Then, just before nightfall, Will returned with Herb Fincher, Joe Simpson, Bo Sloan, and an old pack mule that had never been known to run off. There was an early moon that night, almost a full moon, so they started for the ranch at once. They were afraid to wait until morning because wild stallions had been known to hurt or kill themselves when tied up and left to thrash all night. Shadow was calm now, but if he started to thrash, there would be no way to stop him.

They used the old mule as a kind of walking anchor to make sure that Shadow couldn't run off. They tied the mule and Shadow together at the neck with a strong rope that had about six feet of slack between them. That way both animals could maneuver on the trail without giving Shadow enough rope to play tricks. They kept two other ropes on Shadow's neck, of course, and Rube and Will handled those from their horses. Joe Simpson rode at point to check the trail, and Herb and Bo followed alongside and behind, depending on how wide the trail was. They took it real slow, afraid that something might go wrong.

But it didn't. Strangely, Shadow didn't try the usual tricks. He seemed to know how helpless he was, and he went with them without trouble.

By the time they got home, everything was ready. Uncle Ned and the boys had fixed the mustang corral fixed, with new posts set in along the stream and rebraced like a fortress.

As soon as Shadow saw the gate standing wide and those high rails that walled off such a tiny piece of the world, he balked for the first time. All the freedom he had known made the corral look very small. Halting, he turned his head toward the Winding Stairs. With two ropes tugging on his neck, he looked back and let out such a longing whinny that it seemed to carry for miles. His great nostrils stood out as he whinnied, eyes rimmed white with sorrow. Even when he quit, he resisted an instant longer and kept his ears cocked toward the mountains as if expecting to hear his lead mares answering from the hills. He ignored the urgings of the men around him and kept waiting for that far-off reply. He kept waiting, but there was no answer. None. So at last he let his head be turned and he went with them into the corral.

Word spread fast. People came from miles around to see the stallion.

Pa was as proud of him as Rube was. He talked of breeding him, for even a stallion too wild to ride could sire fine colts. The trouble was that Shadow's bloodline probably wasn't as pure as it appeared. He looked like a purebred Spanish Barb, all right, but odds were against his having a pure line behind him. One of the ranchers called him a "miracle mongrel." If that was true, his colts might—or might not—show fine breeding.

Mom admired Shadow with a smile that made her look much younger and she even went so far as to say that he was the prettiest horse she ever had seen.

Roki and the Indians came, of course. He showed up with his whole outfit and all their children and their medicine man. All afternoon they marveled at the stallion and drummed and sang songs in his honor all night. Having the spirit horse trapped in a corral didn't make Shadow any less important or mysterious to them. Roki and the shaman still said that he burned with a power very old, that he carried the fire of all the wild ones.

At daybreak, Rube and Roki went into the corral to see if the old man could have his wish—to touch the Wind-That-Gallops. The shaman sang low as Roki walked forward. Rube hung back, not knowing what Shadow would do. The stallion wore no hobbles, so he was free to attack if he wanted.

Roki spoke to him softly in his Indian language. All Rube could make out were the words for "wind" and "gallop." Shadow stood his ground until the old man was within a few feet of him, then he backed away a little, but Roki kept talking to him and he put out a hand.

Rube winced as the hand drew nearer. He knew the speed of those teeth and wondered if the shaman's song wasn't some kind of prayer that Roki would survive this. The stallion was close enough now to bite off a nose or a set of fingers in one quick snatch. Yet Shadow stood very still, except for a nervous tremble, and he watched carefully as the old man's hand reached to press the side of his neck.

Roki touched him, and Shadow did not stir. The old man stroked his neck and shoulders, all the while talking to him slow. Shadow waited with a nervous hesitation and let the old man work his medicine.

After stroking Shadow's head in many ways, Roki put his face right up close to the stallion's muzzle and breathed into the horse's nostrils. Shadow shook his head when he did that, but the old man turned away, smiling.

"We have shared breath," Roki told Rube. "I have given him my breath, and he knows me now. I am in him and he is in me. He is ready now to belong to men."

"Does that mean I can ride him now?"

Roki shrugged. "Better wait. . . . This ceremony is good medicine, but I cannot say that he won't kill you."

Before long Shadow broke his fast and began nibbling at Pa's mustang recipe, which relieved Rube. Rube spent hours talking to him. Everything was strange and startling to Shadow: a brush, a bucket, a halter—everything needed some getting used to. But Rube took his time and tried to show in every way how much he cared for the Wind-That-Gallops.

By the end of the week, Shadow would stand while Rube touched and petted him. The stallion never really tried to kick or bite, though Rube was careful not to give him much temptation.

Always Shadow seemed to be studying Rube and this strange way of life closely. He'd stand at the fence for hours, watching as Rube saddled, bridled, and rode other horses around the ranch. Rube hoped that he was learning that horses were treated well at the Tucker spread.

By the end of the next week Rube approached his horse with a hackamore. "Easy, boy. Easy, easy. This isn't any bridle, you know." Shadow looked at the hackamore and stepped back. Rube walked toward him slowly and held it up for the horse to sniff.

"It got no bit, see? It just kinda hugs your nose and lower jaw when I tug on the reins. Just right for a horse with wolf teeth like you."

When Rube reached for Shadow's neck the stallion backed away again.

"Whoa, now. Easy. That's right. Don't you run from me now. Take it easy. Let's put this around your nose— No, don't pull up like that! Take it easy now. Come on." He buckled the strap and kept talking softly. "Just a minute now." Suddenly it was done.

For several days Rube put the hackamore on Shadow and let him wear it around the corral for a few hours just to get used to it. He tied up the reins so they wouldn't slip over the stallion's head when he ate. It wouldn't do for the horse to step on a loose rein and get into a fight with the hackamore—not when things were going so well. So far Shadow had been responding with acceptance to everything Rube introduced him to. Sure he was nervous, but he didn't fight.

It took time and patience to gentle a horse, but Rube felt it was worth it in the long run. You could break a horse in a matter of days, it was true. But that was the problem. The horse was broken in spirit as well. Rube wasn't going to let that happen to the Wind-That-Gallops. He wanted him to keep his pride and dignity—the stallion was worthy of it. It might take two months of coaxing instead of two weeks of rough riding, but Rube was determined to bend Shadow's will, not break it.

Once Shadow was used to the hackamore—he soon wore it as if he had had one all his life—Rube began to train him in its use. He would walk alongside the horse with the reins in one hand, and pull on them gently to stop the horse, or lean the reins against his neck to turn him. If Shadow acted confused or nervous, Rube would just stand next to him and stroke his neck until the quivering stopped.

By the middle of the third week Rube rigged up two sacks of potatoes to get his horse accustomed to carrying weight. Talking quietly, he lowered them onto Shadow's great back. The stallion went rigid and blew through his nostrils with anxiety as soon as he felt the heavy weight. Rube quickly stepped away from him, fearful that the horse might explode into a rearing and kicking fit. Instead Shadow stood stock still, almost as if he was afraid to move.

For a long time the horse and boy stood facing each other. Finally, Shadow seemed to sigh. He walked toward Rube and nudged his pockets for a handout. Rube quickly fed him a carrot and patted his neck. He couldn't believe his good fortune. If this kept up, he would be riding his blue-black stallion in another month or two. It was almost too good to be true.

Herb Fletcher, who had been watching the procedure through the slots in the corral fence, teased, "Why don't you go ahead and bust him? Just saddle him up and see how long you can hold on."

"Nothing doing!" Rube said. "You know very well there's no worse way of introducing man to horse. This isn't some broomtail that needs to be sold at the end of a week!"

"No, but you're going to have to throw a leg over some-day."

"Someday. But I want to gentle him first."

"Gentle him all you want, but I never heard of a full-grown mustang stallion that didn't try to kill the first man to fork him. Did you, Will?"

"Younger ones maybe," Will observed. "But this old—" He shook his head warily. "I don't know. Maybe he won't stomp you too hard."

Rube scowled and let them have their joke, but he kept thinking back to another stallion that he tried to gentle once, a younger stallion, a brown and white pinto with a snort so loud it could be heard hundreds of yards away. They called him Roller-Nose, or Roller for short, because of the way his nose seemed to have rollers rattling inside when he snorted.

In many ways Roller was as gentle as a yard pony, always followed him around, never tried to kick or bite. He'd stand for bridling, for saddling, wouldn't budge even when the cinch was tightened. But try to climb onto him and suddenly he was the meanest bronc on the ranch. He'd let you step into the left stirrup, put your right leg over and settle down, but touching that right stirrup with your boot was like touching off a keg of powder.

It was almost like a game to Roller. He enjoyed it. He had his own rules, drew his own line. He was willing to do anything but let a man ride him. Finally Pa sold him for harness use. Most of the Tucker mustangs went to harness, but still the thought of that handsome pinto pulling a plow or a farmer's wagon for the rest of his life was sad.

Capturing Shadow hadn't done a thing to solve their problem with the bank. There wasn't even a reward since the bounty was for killing him, not catching him; the neighbors reasoned that anybody who caught Shadow alive had reward enough right there. All the mustangs Shadow turned loose still were gone in the wilds, so now instead of having a corral full of broomtails to sell, they had one breathing treasure that nobody wanted to sell. Nobody even wanted to mention the possibility of selling Shadow.

Even Mom never mentioned the bank, and neither did Pa. At last Rube brought it up himself.

"Uh—what about the bank?"

Mom didn't look up from the pan in her lap as she plucked the stems and the little hard tails off small green beans. "Well, we still owe, and they still aim to collect. Why?"

Rube shifted his feet. "I was wondering how—uh— we're going to work that."

"Without selling Shadow, you mean?"

He bobbed his head. "If we can't find the money, the bank could auction off our ranch, right?"

"Not could: they would! But I've been thinking about that." A tiny smile played at her lips. "I think we'll be able to get an extension, one more anyway—"

"Extension?"

"It's like getting another loan, I guess. We've borrowed all we can against the ranch, of course. What we need is something else that we can put up as security, something valuable."

"Shadow?"

"He's all we've got, and nobody can say he isn't valuable."

The idea stirred him uncomfortably. Ever since he tried to fill his Pa's boots and scrape together the bank payments, he'd found himself weighed down by that debt, by the awful possibility of losing their home.

"What if we put up Shadow as security and then can't find the money to pay back the loan? Doesn't that mean we'd lose him too? We could lose Shadow and the ranch both!"

"Not very likely," Mom said. "There's always some risk in doing business. But even the bank won't forget that our biggest problem is over with. Shadow won't be stealing our horses anymore. And now that your father's improving so fast, you'll both be able to go mustanging again. All we need is another bunch to sell. You don't mind catching another bunch, do you?"

Rube grinned slowly. "Guess not."

"Good. Then it's all up to the bank."

"They'll do that, won't they? I mean, you've already talked to Mr. Wade?"

"Not yet. Your father thought you might like to do that."

"Me!"

"Why not? He's your horse. You own him. You'll have to make the deal. Besides, your pa's leg isn't ready for a wagon trip into town. It'd be good for you, too. Give you some experience."

He rubbed his hands on his pants uneasily. He felt kind of shy about going to see old Mr. Wade and talking serious business to him. "What if I say the wrong thing? What do I do if he says 'no'?"

"Oh, I don't think he will. Shadow does have a bad reputation, of course, but Ned tells me you might be riding him soon. Who's going to be afraid of the fire-breathing horse-robber, if young Rube Tucker rides him like any other saddlehorse?"

"What's that got to do with it?"

"See, Mr. Wade won't want to keep Shadow as security without—well—*keeping* him. He's got a fine horse ranch, and I'm sure he'd take good care of him."

"But why can't *we* take good care of him?"

"Well, Rube, when you put up something for security, you can't just do what you want anymore. When we put up the ranch, Mr. Wade put the deed to the ranch in his bank vault. The bank keeps the deed until we pay back the loan. That way we can't sell the ranch to anybody else without settling up the loan first. Don't you see? If he's going to insist on keeping the deed in his vault, then he's going to want to keep Shadow on his ranch. Besides, that way he can breed his mares to Shadow and count the stud fees against the loan."

Rube was staggered. "You mean I spent all that time chasing that stallion and now I've got to turn him over to some banker?"

"I'm sorry, Rube, but at least he'll still be yours!"

"But I won't have him. Not for years!"

"Not years, Rube. Just one year. Just until we pay back the extension."

"Suppose somebody mistreats him? Suppose he comes back mean and vicious?"

"Oh, Rube! Mr. Wade's not a cruel man. I'm sure nothing—"

"Well, I'm not so sure! Suppose we have a bad season? We might lose everything, Shadow and the ranch both!"

"Then what do you want? Want to sell him?"

"No! It's just not fair. I can't believe that a fella can work this hard and then have to turn it all over to some banker who never did anything but sign papers!"

Mom put aside her pan and wheeled on him suddenly, her index finger aimed at his nose. "Now you see here, Rube Tucker. I can show you the books. That bank was nice enough to lend us the money so we could keep going while Pa was hurt, while you were off chasing in the mountains. That bank paid for everything you ate—everything! That's a debt we owe, and I won't hear any of your whining about how unfair it is. It isn't unfair, not even to you. It's hard, I'll grant you. It's real hard. But it isn't unfair."

He withered back with a groan, feeling helpless and defeated to be losing Shadow so soon. He felt a terrible urge to ride that stallion first, to ride him now.

Chapter 12

Rube shouldered out of the narrow doorway of the tack shed with a saddle, blanket, and the new hackamore in his arms.

Ed Simpson looked at him puzzled. "Just a while ago you said it wasn't time."

Rube headed for Shadow's corral.

Ed followed, leading his horse. "You think he's gentled already?"

"We'll see."

"Well, I don't think you think so. I mean, slow down! You act like you want to get killed."

"I just want to ride my horse, that's all." Rube pushed the saddle onto the top rail of the corral, then shook out the blanket as he squinted through the rails at the blue-black stallion. The Wind-That-Gallops perked his ears forward curiously.

Ed moved close. "Rube, wait a while."

"I haven't got a while."

"Well, at least let me get some more of the boys." Ed

started away at a run. "You wait now!" Rube knew that he was running to tell Pa.

Taking the hackamore, he climbed up over the rails and down into the corral. Shadow stood still as Rube adjusted it on his head and drew the reins back over his neck. Rube took up the reins and stroked the stallion along his neck and back, pausing once in a while to put gentle pressure on Shadow's back with the palms of both hands. He kept watching for Shadow to make a move.

It seemed a shame to ruin it all by forcing Shadow too early, but he had to try something. Gentling a horse was just a matter of playing with him, of fooling around with him until he got used to you, but it took a long time unless the horse had a trusting nature.

He had made up his mind to try the stallion bareback first. That way he could slide off quickly if Shadow went crazy. With a saddle he could not get down as fast, and that meant he'd likely stay on just long enough to be thrown off.

Once more he moved his hands along the stallion's back and paused to press down. Since there was no glint of anger in Shadow's eye, Rube pressed harder with his palms, then harder, lifting himself with a little hop. Suddenly he was lying across Shadow's back on his stomach. Yet Shadow didn't try to bite or buck. Instead, he only took a step.

"Whoa, whoa, easy!"

Shadow didn't know what he meant, of course, or didn't care, and took another step. Now Rube had the balance to swing around and straddle him. He paused, waiting for those powerful hind legs to rocket off the ground, for the spine to whiplash under him. But Shadow only took another nervous step.

An awful tingle spread through Rube, a terrifying excitement. He was actually riding the Wind-That-Gallops. For the time being anyway, he was actually astraddle the phantom of the Winding Stairs. It might end any second, and the anticipation made him breathless.

Then he heard the others coming, Will and Ed and Herb and most of the boys. Mom was coming, too, with Uncle Ned and Pa, who was hobbling on crutches with his leg in a cast. All peered through the corral rails. Mom started to call out to him, but Pa shushed her.

Rube could feel the tension spread through Shadow, but then it seemed to fade. He moved his boots inward, touched the stallion very lightly. Shadow didn't budge. He loosened the rein even more and set his teeth as he tried it again, but Shadow didn't start. He only looked confused.

"Guess you don't know what that means," Rube whispered, so he waited until the stallion grew restless and took a step on his own. Then Rube nudged him as he moved and made clicking sounds through his teeth. "That's it. That's what it means."

Shadow kept walking briskly toward the cluster of faces at the rails. All the way Rube didn't know whether to celebrate or hold on tighter. For it couldn't be this easy. All his experience with wild horses told him that Shadow was just waiting for him to relax, waiting for the chance to hurl him at the sky. Yet everything he could read in Shadow's manner told him that it might not happen—at least not now. The stallion was nervous and anxious enough, green and ignorant of leg signals. At the same time he didn't resist the bridle signals or give any clue that he'd refuse to cooperate.

"Well, I'll be," Pa whispered from beyond the fence nearby.

"Didn't he even try to bite?" Will wondered louder.

Rube shook his head to signal that he didn't, and Herb Fincher spoke up. "Then just you wait, pard. He might feel different about saddles."

"You be careful," Mom warned. "We've already got half the family on crutches now."

"I think I'll be all right," Rube said, hoping that he would. "He may not be gentled, but somehow I think he's a—a gentleman."

"A *what?*" Pa exclaimed.

Rube shrugged with one shoulder and turned Shadow away gently. "Never mind. Sounds silly when you try to talk about it. Tell you what. I'll take him around the corral once more, and then we'll try the saddle."

There were nods and grins of encouragement, but deep inside his new joy was turning to sadness. He realized now that he would have been happier in a way if Shadow had turned out to be a devil. If nobody could ride him, then it wouldn't be so painful to send him off to stud on the banker's ranch.

The stallion moved with an easy grace, his feet springing off the ground with snappy steps.

As Shadow and Rube circled back to the group at the fence, Pa grinned proudly. "Say," he called, "wouldn't it be something if you could ride into Minersville next week on that stallion and talk to Mr. Wade yourself? Wouldn't it be something if you showed up riding him?"

Rube nodded sadly. "Yeah," he muttered, "wouldn't that be something?"

Chapter 13

————— ◆◆ —————

"Give you five hundred for him!" somebody yelled, probably joking.

"For this horse?" Rube grinned. He didn't turn, just kept on riding the blue-black stallion down the main street of Minersville. "That kind of money couldn't touch him."

"Perhaps a thousand would!" It was a girl's voice this time, soft but serious.

Rube reined up, and Russian Will and Herb Fincher did the same. He had never seen the pretty young woman who stood on the plank sidewalk. She looked about his own age and was stylishly dressed with a fancy hat and a frilly parasol and white gloves and everything. She wore a soft green dress with puffs at the sleeves and a small bustle. She never even looked at Rube as she moved along the sidewalk, her green eyes admiring the stallion. "He is the most elegant!" Then she glanced up at Rube. "That *is* Shadow, isn't it? The one I've heard about?"

Rube lifted one shoulder in a modest shrug. Shadow perked his ears toward the girl and edged sideways.

As she started to take down her parasol and close it up, Shadow shied back, reared up enough to lift his front hooves off the ground. "Easy, easy."

"I'm sorry!" she said. "I don't suppose he's ever seen a parasol before."

"He's never seen anything like you before. Easy, easy."

She smiled at that. She had black hair, as black as Shadow's. "Somehow I never thought they'd catch him." There was a kind of marveling in her green eyes. "Who made the catch? You?"

"He sure did," Russian Will broke in. "All by hisself, too!" Herb gave him the eye when he said that, and Russian Will's voice trailed away. "Well, we're going up the street to see a man. We'll meet you at the bank." He and Herb rode away quickly.

"My name's Barrett," she told Rube. "Abigail Barrett from Denver. You live around here?"

"Up toward Snake Head Canyon," he motioned. "Name's Rube, Rube Tucker."

"Pleased to meet you, Rube. Now how about a thousand dollars."

Rube frowned and resettled himself in the saddle. "Miss Barrett—"

"Abby."

"Well, Abby, I never even heard of anybody giving that much for a horse! Not around here."

"Would you take less?"

"No!"

"Then how about a thousand?"

Rube tried a good-natured smile and shook his head as he gently pulled some of Shadow's mane out from under the saddleblanket. "Sorry, but I couldn't. Never!"

"But you're a mustanger, aren't you? You catch horses for a living."

"Yeah, but not like this one. There's nothing like Shadow left up there. Not anymore."

"But think, Rube. A thousand dollars. You could buy any ten good horses for that."

"Can't." Rube grinned. "I'm just here to get a loan on him."

"From Mr. Wade?"

He nodded. "You know him?"

"Only on a business basis. I'm here settling up my late father's affairs."

"I'm sorry."

"Oh, that's all right. It's been two years since he died. But anyway, I can tell you something about banks: if you really need the loan, you might not get it."

Rube hardened his face. "Well, I reckon we'll have to see about that." He started to rein away, but she called after him.

"Please wait! I'm sorry." She looked embarrassed. "Oh, I always say the wrong thing. I only meant to warn you, and—would you have lunch with me? I'd like you to."

Rube hesitated, surprised. "Uh, sure! Much obliged. I'm starved."

"I'll be at the hotel dining room. Go see Mr. Wade, and when you're finished join me there."

"Be a pleasure, but I—I won't sell."

She imitated his voice. "Well, I reckon we'll have to see about that." Then she smiled, and he did, too.

"All right then. See you in a few minutes." He wheeled Shadow and rode away toward the bank. He didn't know what to make of her or her warning about the bank, but he couldn't see how there could be any problem. After all, if Abigail Barrett of Denver offered one thousand for Shadow, then he had to be valuable enough to make good security.

He saw Mr. Wade climbing out of a buggy in front of the bank and called to him. The old banker turned and squinted in the midday sun.

"I'm Rube Tucker. If you've got a few minutes, I'd like to talk to you about my father's loan."

Mr. Wade stared at Shadow. "You Seth Tucker's boy?"

"Yes, sir, and this is Shadow." He patted the stallion's neck.

Mr. Wade circled Shadow, but did not come close to him. He bent a little to examine the stallion's fine legs. "So that's the famous stock stealer," he said. "Fine-looking animal. Too bad he's a throwback."

Rube frowned. "What's too bad about that?"

"Well, he's not a purebred, son. He just looks like one."

"But I've caught and sold some colts of his. He sires fine horses."

"Yeah, but they don't look just like him, do they?"

"Well, no, but if he was bred to quality mares—"

"Breeders want pure blood, son. Now what was it you wanted to see me about? Your dad feeling better?"

"Yes, sir, but we need to extend our loan, that's all."

"Again?" The old man looked bothered.

"But we've got some mighty fine security here," Rube said quickly. He rubbed the stallion's mane. "He's worth a fortune."

"Oh, I'm sure he could *cost* you a fortune," he said, his meaning half-hidden in a smirk. "What'd you have in mind?"

The tone of his voice made Rube uneasy. "Well, if you'll extend the loan, you can take Shadow as security and breed him on your ranch."

"My ranch?"

"Yes, sir. He'll sire good colts—"

"And run off with my mares," Wade interrupted. He

shook his head. "Now that'd be putting the fox among the chickens, wouldn't it?"

"Well, look, if you're afraid to have him on your ranch, then we'll keep him at ours and you can bring your mares over when you want. We'll work it any way you want."

"How about meeting your payments on time? That's what I want."

"But that's day after tomorrow, and we don't have the money."

"Why not?"

"Well, we had this big bunch of mustangs corralled at the ranch, but—"

"What happened?"

"Well, we lost 'em."

"Lost 'em! How?"

Rube looked down. "Well, Shadow ran 'em off, but—"

"See what I mean?"

"But—but that was before! Now he's broke to saddle and everything. He won't be any trouble."

Mr. Wade smiled that away. "Come on, son, someday that stallion's going to look at the mountains and feel the wind in his tail and he's going to wonder why he ever left. That's the day you'll lose every mare on the place."

Rube's chest tightened until he was almost panting for breath. "Then you won't do it? You're sure?"

"I'm sure," the banker said. "Now I know you're in a spot, but I can't risk having that stallion on my place. He's a stock thief. And if you keep him on your spread, then he'll just steal your stock someday, so the risk's a bad one for either of us. Understand?"

"Then what are we going to do?"

"Well, I don't want to foreclose. I'd hate to see you lose your ranch. Are you sure you can't raise the two hundred dollars you need?"

Rube felt sick. "I'm sure."

The banker shrugged. "All right then, tell you what. I don't really want to, but—if it'll help you out—I'll give you two hundred for the stallion." He made it sound like a big favor.

Rube stiffened, eyes narrowing. "I thought you said you wouldn't risk having him on your place."

"Not as a boarder, no. But if I owned him, I guess I could build a special stall or something."

"But two hundred sure isn't much."

"It's about double what he's worth!"

"Abigail Barrett offered me a thousand dollars!"

Mr. Wade smirked. "She was pulling your leg, son."

"She wasn't."

"Then I suggest you sell to her. Go ahead and take her up on it. Go ahead. She'll back down."

"I doubt it."

"Then you won't have any trouble at all saving the ranch, will you?" He smiled as he turned away. "See you day after tomorrow."

Rube burned slowly. The old man seemed so sure he'd own the stallion soon. Two hundred dollars! It seemed like nothing when talking about Shadow, but when it came to finding that much in cash, it seemed like a lot more. He had just two days, and there was no way to catch more mustangs and sell them that quickly. Even their saddlehorses, buckboard, and harness were borrowed against, so there was nothing they could sell for two hundred dollars.

He felt sick to his stomach as he turned back toward the hotel to see Abby. Now she was his only chance: he'd have to ask her for the loan.

Chapter 14

———◆◆———

He met Herb and Will there on the street and gave them the bad news. They promised to take care of Shadow while he went to lunch with Abby and wished him good luck.

"I may need it," he said. "Funny, but I was hungry a while ago."

"Banking's bad for ya," Will said.

"Well, I'm not through yet. Now I reckon I've got to ask her for the money."

"Tell her she's got pretty eyes," Will said. "I always tell 'em they've got pretty eyes. They like that."

Rube smirked. "Two hundred dollars worth?" He went into the Hotel Minersville. It was the town's biggest building, one of the few in town with wallpaper and carpets and properly finished woodwork.

Abby was at a corner table in the dining room looking out a window at Herb and Will walking Shadow back and forth. A waiter brought them oysters on the halfshell —the first oysters Rube had ever seen.

"Oysters in Minersville!" He was amazed.

"You'll like them," Abby said. "Try some of this sauce."

He risked one—and liked it. "Where did they come from?"

"I brought a barrel of them on my train."

"You've got a *train?*"

"Well, not a whole train. Just a few private cars."

"Oh . . . Well, these are good."

She seemed pleased. "See why I have a weakness for oysters? We've had them in Denver ever since I can remember. They come packed in barrels with their 'mouth sides' upright. That way the crew can feed them by pouring sea water mixed with food down through the barrel. As long as they do that often enough and keep the barrel cool, the oysters stay alive. Well, did you get the loan?"

Rube shook his head.

"What are you going to do now?"

"Ask you for it," he said seriously. "We need two hundred dollars to keep the bank from foreclosing on our ranch." He held his breath. "You can have my stallion to back up the loan."

She did not look at him. "I'm no banker, Rube."

"But you could lend us two hundred dollars! It means our home!"

"Don't you know anyone else? Some friend or neighbors?"

"No, we've tried. Times are hard around here right now, and nobody's got the slack. Nobody!"

A chill crept into her tone. "Well, Rube, the bank's in that business. That's what banks are for. If they won't lend it to you, if your friends and neighbors won't lend it to you, then how can you ask me?"

"Because you're my last chance."

"Well, I'm sorry, but I have to make it a flat rule. If you had any idea how many people ask me for loans all the time, you'd be ashamed to bring it up. I'm bothered all the time by people trying to borrow money, and I don't want to be bothered by you."

He sat back in his chair and kept his mouth shut. She acted as if she wanted him to apologize, but he wouldn't do that. "If it was your family's place, you'd be doing the same."

"Oh, I don't know," she said. "If my family were in the horse business and if they needed two hundred dollars to save the ranch, I think I might be ... big enough to sell my own horse. Even though he was my favorite. That would be the grown-up thing to do."

"I can't do that. There's got to be some other way."

"Why?"

He was surprised that she could ask. "Abby, it isn't just that he's my favorite. Shadow's the finest thing ever to come my way. He's just what I always wanted, what I always dreamed of. It's a pure miracle that I ever caught him. I just can't tell you how much he means to me."

"That's exactly how I feel," Abby said. "We're not so different, you and I."

"Then share him with me! Just lend us enough to save the ranch. You can keep him till the debt's paid. That's fair, isn't it?"

"Not to me. Maybe I'm spoiled. All right, I'll admit I am. But it wouldn't be the same, don't you see? It wouldn't be the same just having him for a little time." She looked down at her plate. "I don't think I could stand that."

"You mean, you couldn't stand to give him back?"

At last she nodded.

Rube sighed. "Well, I guess I can't fault you for wanting to own him. That's what I wanted ever since I first laid eyes on him."

"Love at first sight?"

He blushed, but agreed.

"Then we're not so different, are we? That's exactly what happened to me."

"But, Abby, you can't know how much he means to me!"

She looked indignant to hear that. "Oh can't I? What makes you think I can't love him as much as you do?"

"It's just that I laid awake so many nights. I spent so many days and months chasing him through rocks and snow. I nearly got killed!"

"But that's the business you're in. You're in the business of catching wild horses, and I'm not. All I've got is money, so let's trade."

"You act like there's another one up there someplace. But there isn't. Not like Shadow!"

"So I've heard, but what does that mean, if you lose your ranch?"

He let his eyes harden. "You've got me in a tough place, don't you?"

"Me? Oh, Rube! It's hardly my fault your friends and neighbors and bank can't lend you the money. I never offered to be your banker. All I did was offer you a—a fabulous price for your fabulous horse. That's all."

"But you could lend us the money, if you really wanted to. We'd pay you interest and everything."

"I don't want your money," she told him coolly. "I just want your horse."

"But I can't! I can *not* sell him!"

"Because you love him too much?"

"Right."

"Well, I love him too much to borrow him, don't you see? I couldn't stand to have him and then give him back. So what else can I do? I offered you a *good* price. If I didn't love him so much, I wouldn't offer so much."

"You keep talking about love and money at the same time."

Her green eyes sharpened. "I'm sorry that offends you. Look, Rube, if you think I'm trying to take advantage of you somehow, if you think I'm trying to cheat you, then perhaps we'd better forget all about it."

"No, wait. I didn't say you're trying to cheat me. It's just that . . ." He ran out of words.

"You love your horse more than your ranch," she said. "Well, I can understand that, I suppose." Then she shrugged. "I'm sure your folks'll understand."

Rube simmered. This spoiled girl with her frosty manner was his last chance. He wanted to get mad, but he didn't dare. He had to save the ranch, but his mind scrambled like a cat in a sack, clawing to find some way out of this, some other way than selling Shadow.

When they went out after lunch, Shadow cocked his ears toward him, his expression brightening like a bored pup glad to see his master come out to play. He shifted his hooves, anxious to get away from Will and Ed.

Rube introduced them to Abby, who said, "Let's take him down by the depot. I'll have my porter get out my sidesaddle. I think I'd better ride him before we close the deal."

Shadow looked puzzled as they cinched on the strange saddle with the single stirrup. He seemed to be questioning Rube, trying to understand what was happening.

Soon Abby tucked the toe of her high-buttoned shoe into the stirrup and pulled herself up. Her right knee crooked over the special horn in front and her left supported her from the stirrup. It looked like a mighty unhandy arrangement, but it was the only way that a lady could ride with long skirts on, and all ladies wore long skirts while riding.

Her hair was as black as Shadow's. Somehow her black hair and white skin seemed to match the black and white markings of the Wind-That-Gallops. It made them look very special together, like some kind of matched set.

As the porter handed up her riding crop, Rube stepped forward and snatched it away. "Give me that. I never hit him, and you'd better not." He grasped the hackamore for an instant and scratched the side of Shadow's head, as he looked him in the eye and whispered, "Behave now, hear?"

He turned loose and let her take him. She handled herself confidently enough, reined gently enough, and Shadow obeyed, even in his confusion. Rube stood there with his hands in his pockets, watching as she worked the stallion in brisk figure eights, first one way, then the other.

When she swung back closer again, her face was aglow. "He's wonderful!" she called. "I can hardly believe he was ever wild."

"Well, he was," Rube said. "He was." And that made him feel even worse. For Shadow had never needed breaking really. He let Rube ride him, as a matter of trust or friendship. So now that Shadow behaved like any other saddlehorse, he was being sold like any other saddlehorse.

Some reward, Rube thought. This was what he got for being so gentle, dignified, and tame. What a double cross!

Maybe Shadow knew it too. Always before the big stallion's gaze had touched him with something like strong trusting friendship, but the obsidian gem that eyed him now showed only sadness, shame, and disappointment. Even betrayal. Shadow looked away from him.

"How about it?" Abby asked. "It's a deal, isn't it?"

Rube lowered his eyes and nodded slowly. "I reckon he's yours."

Chapter 15

For a while it seemed as if a great big hole had been carved out of his life. Yet slowly he began to feel better as word trickled back from Denver way, word that Abby and Shadow were getting along like old trail partners. Riding the stallion through the streets of the city, she created the public sensation she always yearned for.

She kept her promises to Rube. She didn't change Shadow at all, didn't shoe him or crop his long mane or tail. She hired a French trainer and a groom to pamper him and had a special railroad car built and padded to make a rolling stable for him.

She took him with her everywhere. Shadow was always the center of attention, a captured king, treated like a king. He never gave any trouble, so that had to mean that he didn't mind being Abby's horse.

Rube couldn't flatter himself by pretending that Shadow missed him. It was true that most tamed stallions turned into one-man or one-woman horses, but he had owned Shadow for less than a month, so it was plain Shadow had adopted Abby as his sole owner.

As for Rube, well, for him even mustanging lost some of its glory. The old game just wasn't the same any more, not like the old days when he chased that wind spirit through the rocks. Now it seemed almost too easy to round up the scrubs that roamed the foothills of the Winding Stairs. After chasing the wind, everything else looked mud footed.

Red and Firelight were still impossible to catch, for there's no mustang harder to catch than a saddlehorse gone wild. Such a horse knew all the tricks and wouldn't be trapped.

The sorrel that took over Shadow's manada wasn't worth catching. He was strong, but ugly, badly scarred from fights with Shadow and other stallions. Most of his ears had been chewed off.

In the long chase most of the sorrel's band gave out and were captured, a few at a time. Rube and the boys caught all the colts, then the mares, and finally only Red and Firelight and their scruffy stallion got away.

One by one, they cleaned out the other wild bunches in the area. Moving south, the Tucker outfit ran an entire herd into a trap and caught forty-three horses at once. Many were only colts, but Pa made a deal with a neighbor who could raise them on fenced range, so even the colts brought a good price.

The bank was no problem now, for Mr. Wade had no hard feelings about losing Shadow to Abby, and Tucker Ranch had so many boxes that soon neighbors were taking care of the extras.

They did so well that one evening Pa returned from town and gave Rube a little book from the Bank of Minersville. "It's a savings account," he explained somewhat shyly as he stood in the doorway of Rube's bedroom.

"Shadow was your horse, so now that we're on our feet again, your mother and I want you to—well, to have the thousand dollars, at least." He showed him the entry inked on the first yellow pages: "July 30, 1898: $1,000.00."

"It's yours," Pa said. There was a trace of anxiety and shame in the way he talked. "I know it'll never replace Shadow, but the money's yours and we want you to have it. We know how hard it was for you, and—and we're awful sorry you had to . . . We want you to know we're proud of you."

Rube thanked him. But when he looked in his bankbook he thought that no inked figures anywhere could be "worth" as much as Shadow.

Next morning a carriage rolled up the road that led to Tucker Ranch. The liveryman from Minersville was driving, and inside was Abby Barrett. She looked badly shaken. "He's gone! Shadow's gone! Escaped!"

"Escaped?" Rube frowned as he helped her down. "What happened?"

She was trembling slightly. "Oh, Rube, I don't know why he'd—I treated him so well, but—" She paused to collect herself. "It happened in Idaho. I heard this awful commotion in the stable. It sounded like somebody was tearing down the place with sledgehammers! By the time I got outside, part of the stable wall was gone—and so was Shadow."

"You mean to say he kicked his way out?"

She reached into the carriage, brought out a scrap of splintered planking, and showed him the dented impressions on the wood. "My blacksmith says Shadow did that. From the inside. Rube, we have to find him."

"Well, why come to me? Hadn't you better look in Idaho first?"

She shook her head fast. "You don't understand. He's on his way here! A rancher on the Idaho line saw him. He's been running this way ever since he left my stable. He must be here by now."

"You mean up there," he muttered, looking away toward the Winding Stairs. He felt his heart quicken and the old temptation tug at him.

"Help me catch him and I'll give you a thousand-dollar reward," Abby said. "When do we start?"

Rube squinted at her. "We?"

"Well, he's my horse! Even if he's loose, he's still my horse."

"But that's no excuse for slowing us down. Look, that's no city park up there."

"I can ride," she snapped.

"Sure, but how long? Can you ride all day? And all day the next? And the next?"

She frowned at him. "That's my problem. I can ride, and if I'm going to pay for this expedition, then I'm going along."

"You'll be no help, Abby."

"Just call it looking after my investment. Now come on, Rube. I'll pay ten dollars a day, whether you catch him or not, but I'm going along."

"To make sure I earn it?"

"That's right. Now let's get started. My saddle and things are right here." She reached in the carriage.

They stared at each other. He didn't like the way she tried to boss him around, but there was no use pretending that he didn't want to go after Shadow. There was nothing else he'd rather do, with or without Abby Barrett.

Finally, Rube reached for her things in the carriage. "At ten dollars a day," he grumbled, "you could slow us down enough to cost yourself a fortune. You might spoil all chance of catching him. And, I'll tell you right now, we'll probably never catch him anyway. So how's that looking after your investment?"

She flushed angrily. "You just can't imagine, can you? You can't imagine that somebody else could love that horse as much as you do."

By noon they were on their way, Rube and Pa, with Abby, Will, Ed, Joe, Herb, and Gibb Russell and Bo Sloan.

Abby made a strange-looking mustanger in her lady's riding clothes. She wore a top hat with sash tied around it like a wide hatband and the brim folding up close on either side. Her long skirt and short jacket were of black serge, with the jacket fitting snug at the waist. A white frill sash made a tie at her throat.

All wondered how she'd do in the roughs. She couldn't be shaken off the left side, of course, for there she had all her support, but falling off the right side would be easier, since her right leg was crooked around that special saddlehorn and not planted down in a stirrup. Rube thought that Indian women had a better idea in riding astraddle like a man. But Abby wouldn't even consider it.

She rode a horse named Jimmy that was never known to lag or play tricks. She was determined to show everybody what a horsewoman she was, even if it killed her. She could make Jimmy do anything she wanted, but she wasn't used to riding hour after hour. Before long her legs and lower back began to tire and grow sore. By the second morning she was very stiff, but denied it. Even though everybody could see the pained way she moved when she climbed from her horse, she would not admit that she hurt.

She was surprised how far they had to ride before sighting horses. They found a few, but there was no sign of Shadow. Then, on the fifth day out, they came across the body of a dead stallion. It was the sorrel.

Rube's mount grew jumpy at the smell of horse blood, so Rube squeaked down and handed the reins to Joe Simpson. Will dismounted and walked over with him.

Flies buzzed around, but the body was too fresh to smell. The stallion lay in a small clearing, his throat torn open. His blood made a dark, dust-covered puddle in the dirt. Two sets of hoofprints cut up the ground all around and there was no sign of any other animal, so it had to have been a stallion duel.

"Must've been some fight," Rube said. "When do you think it happened?"

"Yesterday maybe."

"Think it was Shadow?"

Will shrugged and scratched his beard. "Wait a minute." He reached to the stallion's muzzle and turned back the upper lip. "Looky there."

Inside the mouth, between the lip and the teeth, there was a scattering of short, loose hairs torn from the hide of the other stallion. They were black and shiny—Shadow's hair.

Rube looked up at the hills around him and he walked back to Abby and the others. "It was him all right. Shadow's reclaimed his territory."

"And his mares," Abby added. "That'll make him easier to follow, won't it?"

"Some," Pa said. "More hooves leave more sign."

"But look where they went!" Rube motioned toward the

tracks that wound up the mountainside toward the pass. "He's got Red and Firelight leading now and he's gone home." He tried to put a warning tone in that word *home*, but Abby ignored it.

"Well, at least we've got a trail to follow."

Rube looked to his pa, a sort of "help me" look, as he went to mount up.

Pa cleared his throat. "Uh, Miss Barrett, I had a hard time explaining this to Rube once, but you've got to understand. Shadow's home is up beyond that pass over there, up in the high roughs where no mustanger can do any real good. Honest! We've tried it. Rube's tried it. The Indians tried it. Lots of mustangers tried—"

"Does that mean *we* shouldn't?" Abby asked scornfully.

"Honest," Pa said, "we don't catch horses up there ourselves. Not up there!"

"Maybe he'll come down again this winter," Rube said quickly.

Her eyes flared. "This winter!"

"I know how you feel," Rube said. "That's just how I felt about it, but Pa's not kidding you. Next winter we'll have a chance."

"I want him now," she said, as if saying that would get it done.

Rube squinted at her. "Now?"

"*Now!*" She glared at him.

Pa tried to ease in. "Miss Barrett, you can't—It'd be a miracle if we *ever* catch him! Don't you see?"

"We can start now."

"Sounds like me," Rube muttered with a grin. "I used to be hard-headed like you, Abby, but he's telling you the truth. We'd be wasting your money up there, that's all."

"Isn't ten dollars a day enough for this outfit?"

"Sure, but look," Rube said. "Last year three whole outfits of mustangers threw together and worked those mountains at the same time. Three outfits ganged up on him, but they didn't get close." He held up gloved fingers. "Think of it. *Three* whole outfits!"

Abby lifted her chin, lips pursed tightly. "All right," she said, "how much would it cost to hire *six* whole outfits?"

Chapter 16

—◆—

At first, Rube thought it might be hard to round up that many experienced mustangers, especially now that so many had been forced to retire. Abby sent telegrams to all the oldtimers who had chased Shadow last year, and to all the others Pa knew of. A few of those who had already tried it backed off, but others wanted to try again, especially now that their expenses would be paid.

The Candice brothers of West Texas were long retired, but they sent word that they were coming with two extra hands. The Double Bar outfit from Wyoming, the Boatright boys of Oregon, and the Miller outfit from Nevada were on their way by train, anxious to have one last try at a great mustang stallion.

Roki's outfit came down from the Cloud Cascades along with the medicine man and with extra horses for men and supplies. Even among the Indians there was a new excitement, for it seemed to everybody that with all those mustangers working together, somebody ought to catch the Wind-That-Gallops.

By the time the various outfits arrived, Pa had all the supplies purchased and ready to be loaded on packhorses and the family mule. They had plenty of mounts for the other four outfits, mountain horses, former mustangs, tough and rugged.

Abby bought herself an army Sibley tent, complete with a portable stove to warm it, and a case of tinned goods so she wouldn't have to chew jerky all the time. She brought along a chubby woman named Mavis to cook and wash and look after her.

When everything was ready, they headed for the Winding Stairs, the largest force of experienced mustangers Rube had ever heard of—all to chase one stallion and his harem of mares.

Shadow's harem was small now, for he won only five mares when he killed the sorrel stallion. If the battle had happened earlier in the summer, Shadow wouldn't have claimed that many, for at one time the sorrel lost all his mares, except for Red and Firelight. No telling how he had found the other three before Shadow caught up to him.

When the mustangers reached the Winding Stairs, they spread out and made five different camps, hoping to drive Shadow from one to another. The Miller outfit from Nevada brought something different, some signaling machines called heliographs that they'd learned to use in the Army.

The heliographs used sunlight to flash signals from one place to another. They were three-legged machines, fitted with a shutter mirror and sight and adjustments for angling the sunbeam just right to throw the flash where they wanted. They worked better than pocket mirrors because often it was difficult to make sure that every flash from a pocket mirror went in the right direction. The heliographs also had keys like telegraph keys so the operators could tap out Morse code.

The Miller boys were good with their equipment, but

unfortunately their machines didn't work as well in the Winding Stairs as in the desert and on the plains. On open ground they could signal riders to head southeast or northwest, and it was easy to do: just point their horses and go. But in the Winding Stairs, where there were no maps and no place names, mustangers had to ride very crooked trails that split and wove between giant rocks and mountains. Simple directions were impossible.

Meanwhile, Shadow and his band proved as crafty as always. Red and Firelight were experienced leaders in this country. They outguessed every trap and led the band up and around the narrows. They found trails that men on horseback couldn't follow, and they seemed to delight in tempting the men into danger. They played like mountain sheep on the steep granite, always out of reach.

Sometimes at night, when other wild horses would have been glad for a little rest, Shadow would take his mares on moonlight gallops into the high roughs. By morning they were miles from where they started, and all the lookouts would be straining to find horses among the trees and boulders. It might take a day or more to find them again. Once they were found, Shadow would disappear again.

"We'll get him," Earl Candice kept telling Abby. "Wild horses ain't got a chance in the long run because Nature makes 'em stake out a spread and stick to it. He's got a mighty strange spread here, I'll allow, but as long as he keeps circling back to the same thirty-mile area, he's got to wear down eventually."

Nobody was saying how long "eventually" might be, of course. But with so many mustangers in the mountains, it seemed impossible for Shadow to keep dodging all of them. Abby promised a fifty-dollar bonus to the first man to capture even one of Shadow's mares, so the race picked up new speed.

Two days later one of Shadow's mares went lame, a yellow one with a dark line down the middle of her back. Si Jameson caught her with no trouble and collected his bonus, though Abby wasn't very happy about the way it happened. Roki told her that he could sell her many lame mares for fifty dollars apiece, but she didn't seem to appreciate his funning.

At Roki's suggestion they moved three of the campsites, hoping to camp nearer places where Shadow would pass. Gradually, as the men became more familiar with the area, they began to hem in the stallion.

The Candice brothers gave Shadow a good chase one morning, then the Jameson boys took over that afternoon. The Boatright boys found them early the next day and kept them moving until they neared the Indian camp. So when night fell and the moon rose, Roki's Indians followed them very slowly. At dawn they ran them hard again, and just when Shadow probably thought he had shaken off the last of Roki's riders, the Tucker outfit got word by heliograph that the Wind-That-Gallops was headed their way.

"You sure you want to go?" Rube asked as he cinched up Abby's sidesaddle. "He'll fight if he's cornered."

"I'll let you take the chances, don't worry." She pulled on black leather gloves, her riding crop tucked under her arm. "Is your Indian friend coming with us?"

"Kehoni?" Rube smiled at the question. "He missed his turn with Roki." He twisted back to see Kehoni rushing to saddle one of the packhorses. "He's been waiting for this a long time. Longer than you."

They left Mavis in camp with a rifle and everybody else rode out to head off Shadow. They climbed to the ridge which Shadow was supposed to be following. But no sooner did they get there than they spotted the stallion and his four mares breezing through the valley below. The wild bunch galloped right past their camp!

By the time the mustangers came down the hillside, Shadow had a good headstart across the wildflower meadows that led up the valley. Yet the Tucker outfit had fresh horses under them, so they flayed hard to catch up. They raced across meadows where flowers spread for miles, dodging the darkest green places where thick mud lay.

They skirted a glacier lake that wore a patch of sky on its surface, a still image of white puffy clouds amid the blue. They ducked among boulders and trees at its edge, then dashed through a stream that gurgled down toward the lake. Everywhere the air smelled of evergreens.

Shadow seemed to let them get closer, as if to get a better look at Abby and the rest. When his mares started up a hillside, he whirled at the base and threw up his head and snorted loud at the riders that followed. Rube thought he looked surprised to see him and Abby and Pa and the other Tucker hands.

Abby called out to him, but he didn't look twice. He only spun on his hind legs and made for the top, black hooves gobbling up great lengths with every bound.

"Shadow!" Abby called. "Shadow, it's me!"

Rube pitied her, remembering how it felt when he first tried to call Red back to him, how it felt when he screamed his throat raw calling her. Shadow never so much as cocked an ear.

The wild ones led them along hillsides, then down into meadows and back to the roughs. As the sun dipped low, Shadow made his band climb higher to a long ridge where the rock lay stacked in broad benches and shelves. The mustangs were tiring now. They were slowing down and letting their lead distance melt away.

For the first time on this trip, Rube untied his lariat.

Firelight guided the band along one of the high benches, then up a steep path that angled fifty feet to the next shelf above. Shadow followed them up and out of sight there. Rube could see, as he rode, that those higher shelves led up and along the ridge which stretched away toward a peak.

The mustangers mixed and strung out on the shelf. Joe Simpson rode to point, with Rube after him, followed by Pa and Will and Abby and Kehoni. The others weren't far behind.

"My turn, pard!" Joe Simpson yelled as he reined his gelding ahead of Rube and pointed him up the steep pathway. Joe's lariat was ready, his teeth clenched in a grin. His snipe-nosed bay gained the incline in jarring lurches almost to the top.

Following along behind on Crazy, Rube kept glancing up to the left, up past his hatbrim at the edge of that shelf where Shadow disappeared. He wondered if Shadow had made much distance by now, but then he heard Joe yell: "Wha—Hey!"

Shadow loomed at the trail's head, flashed into view just as Joe's horse struggled to gain the edge. The stallion blocked the way, attacked with teeth and forefeet, ears laid back and eyes aflame. Joe never had a chance to twirl or throw, for his startled gelding shied back, white-eyed, and stumbled off the trail, falling. Joe threw himself at the mountain, put out his arms and caught rock, while his bay went tumbling down the slope some fifty feet to the bottom shelf. Stirrups flapped out wide as the horse rolled, and when the poor gelding hit bottom, he couldn't get up.

Joe was scrambling to a place where he could catch his breath. "Look out!" he gasped. "Don't go up there!"

Rube's horse had already decided that: Crazy planted himself suddenly on the steep path, just hopped and clutched, gripping the mountain with all four hooves. His legs quivered, unable to move without slipping backward.

Rube glanced all around, desperate to do something, but not knowing what. He couldn't turn around here, couldn't get back down, couldn't get down at all without falling. And Shadow was still up there, waiting.

He saw the stallion peek over the edge, saw the long white star, those angry eyes. Crazy saw him too and flinched all over.

"Whoa, easy!" Rube made a show of twirling his rope, even though he dared not throw it, and as soon as Shadow saw that loop swing, he ducked back out of sight again. Maybe running away!

Rube hesitated, anxious to take this chance but not knowing if Shadow was really running away or just getting ready for another bushwhack. Still, he had little choice. It was climb or fall now, so he put heels to Crazy. "Come on." The gelding didn't want to try it; Rube kicked him again and again. "Come on!"

Crazy's hooves slid backward a few times and his eyes grew bigger with every slip, but then he caught a firmer hold and began to throw himself up and up.

"What are you doing?" Joe hollered. "Shadow's up there!"

Rube grated his teeth and kept twirling that rope as he rode to the top. He hoped that not being surprised would count for something, that swinging that loop might keep Shadow back. Then he reached the top and saw Shadow a dozen yards away. The stallion seemed to be checking the progress of his mares up the next incline, but he saw Rube at once and braced himself, head high, eyes alert, tail standing at a high angle.

Crazy balked at first sight of the stallion, so Rube didn't wait. He threw the lariat.

Shadow watched its flight with a rope-wise gleam, then threw his head to the ground, just put his nose right down on the dirt so no loop could close on his neck. The rope flapped on his shoulder and slid off to the ground, useless. Then his eyes brightened, his ears folded back, his wolf teeth opening as if to say, "Gotcha now!" And he sprang forward at a charge.

Rube didn't have time to do anything, for Crazy wasn't about to tangle with that stallion again. The gelding threw himself up and twisted away so quickly that Rube's hat flew off to hang by the chinstrap. He nearly came out of the saddle and before he could make sure that he was on firmly, Crazy was plunging back down the trail with the rope trailing after.

Yet Pa was in the way! He was starting up the path, riding up to help, and he couldn't back down fast enough. Crazy kept rushing down in a panic, but fortunately Pa's gelding still had his head about him. Pa's horse looked to the side, saw he could make it and sprang away from the ledge like a bighorn sheep. It was eight feet or better to the shelf below, so the horse put his forelegs out stiff, took up part of the shock there, and when his hind legs hit, he bounced into a short run. Pa was all over him trying to stay on. When those forefeet hit, Pa went forward out of the saddle and saved himself only by hugging the horse's neck. It took him a second to get back on right and stop his horse again.

Abby was catching up as Rube reached the bottom. "What are you doing?" she screamed. "Go get him!"

Even before Rube could answer, Kehoni dodged past on his borrowed pony and charged up that path as if nothing had happened, his lariat whirling all the way. "No!" Rube hollered, yanking Crazy around. "Kehoni, don't! Kehoni!"

Joe yelled at him, too, from his perch on the incline, but Kehoni didn't slow. Then, just as his pony scrambled to the top of the trail, Shadow wheeled up there, put his head down and kicked. Both hooves drove into the pony's skull and neck, making a hollow noise like a crockery jug breaking on soft ground. Kehoni's horse dropped like a dead thing, just turned loose all at once and collapsed and rolled. Kehoni spilled from the saddle, almost got caught up in it, but managed to get free and slide. His horse fell in a heap at the bottom, dead.

As Kehoni and Joe tried to help each other down the slope, Shadow came to the rim and reared high. He tossed his shiny mane, showed his wolf teeth, and whinnied his dare at all of them. He dared them to come up, dared them, and he made boxing motions with his front hooves before standing down again.

Furious, Abby turned her horse around and around. "Well?" she demanded, as the men gathered in. "What are you going to do? Just look at him?"

He was so close, but so impossible to approach.

"He's right there" Abby fumed. "Isn't anybody going after him?" Her gaze flew from face to face, searching for somebody who would try, and the men's reluctance only made her more angry. "All right," she cried. "He's never hurt me, so follow me!" She yanked Jimmy around and urged him at the trail.

"Whoa, wait!" Rube put heels to old Crazy and rode up quickly to catch her bridle. "I said wait!"

"Let me go."

"What for? So you can die?"

Pa rode up on her other side. "Come on, Miss. He's got us here, don't you see?"

"Then what are we going to do? Just let him go?"

"For now," Pa said.

"What?"

"Well, it's getting late and, besides, we can't get him here. Come tomorrow he'll be somewhere else."

"That's what I mean! We'll have to start all over."

"No." Pa wagged his head. "We did our day's work. We wore 'em out pretty good. But we'll never get him by trying this. The day we get him, we'll have all the advantages, not him, so let's quit for now."

"Before somebody else gets hurt," Rube added fast, and suddenly everybody startled when a revolver banged. It was Joe Simpson finishing off his gelding.

"Joe and Kehoni are pretty skinned up," Pa told her. "And we've lost two horses. We can't afford to play 'king of the mountain' where he's bound to win. That's not how you catch wild horses."

Abby glanced grimly at the shelf above and saw that Shadow was out of sight now. Without a word, she reined away and swatted Jimmy into a slow lope, heading back toward camp.

Poor Jimmy, Rube thought. He had to feel sorry for any creature that had to answer to Abby Barrett. It was sad she couldn't figure out anything better to do with her frustration than burn it up getting mad; certainly it didn't seem to make her feel better.

Some of the men went back with Abby, but Rube, Pa, Will, and Herb stayed behind to help Joe and Kehoni with their saddles and gear. Joe was limping with a twisted foot and he had a big gash on one hand. Kehoni was scratched up pretty badly too, with big bruises on a leg and elbow.

Kehoni went to Pa with a shy, sad look and said, "I owe you a horse."

"No, you don't," Pa replied sharply. He looked after Abby and beat dust out of his hat. "She told you to ride up that trail. She's paying expenses, so let her."

"But I borrowed him, and I lost him—"

"On her orders. That's expenses." He looked around at Rube. "I just wish I could teach you boys to be a little more scared of that stallion!"

"Don't worry," Rube muttered, "Shadow's a pretty good teacher."

Nobody thought much about it when Shadow couldn't be found the next day. But after four days went by without a sign of him, everybody was worrying. The trackers tried in vain to pick up a trail. Apparently, Shadow and his band had walked for miles on the high rock ridges where they left little sign. At last they found some tracks and followed them, even though Roki said they looked odd. A full day later they found the horses that made the trail: young bachelor stallions that roamed the hills together because they had no manadas of their own.

They searched every part of the Winding Stairs for another week, but there was no sign of Shadow and his mares.

"I don't believe it," Abby fumed, as she paced around the campfire. "I just don't believe it. Why would he leave his territory?"

"Maybe we ran him off." Rube snapped twigs and arranged them in the fire to hurry the coffee. Pa and the others were off somewhere since nobody liked to be around Abby when she was boiling herself into a stew.

"I've got to admit this is some kind of problem we never heard of before. But then we never filled the mountains with so many men before. Maybe he's just too crowded."

"Oh, so now it's too many men. First, it's not enough men. Now you say it's too many. What an excuse!"

"It's no excuse. Just put yourself in his place a minute. He can't eat, can't sleep without men tracking him and running him. Everyplace he goes, there's another bunch waiting. Put yourself in his place. Would you stand for that?"

Her eyes blazed. "When I think of what I've stood for! I ache all over, have for weeks. I smell like smoke. And the money! Do you have any idea how much this nightmare has cost?"

"Well, you wanted it."

"But I thought you'd catch my horse!"

Rube shook a bug off his coffee cup and poured some. "I don't know, Abby. I reckon he doesn't want to be your horse anymore."

She came around the fire and glared down at him. "Well, he *is* my horse, Rube Tucker, and don't you forget it. I don't lose ownership just because he ran away. He's still mine, whether you catch him this year or next or next. Understand?"

"Oh, I understand," he said. "I just don't think you do. Maybe he doesn't want to be your horse or my horse or anybody's horse. Maybe that's why he ran off to begin with."

She wouldn't hear it. "What difference does that make? He's still mine."

"But I'm trying to make you see his part of it, that's all. Look, he tried. He tried. He put up with you and me and with that fancy French groom of yours. He ate his oats, did everything you wanted. He did it all, tried it all, had it all—"

"I loved him," she interrupted.

"Yeah, well, that too. Maybe he enjoyed it, too. I'm not saying he didn't. But what's love compared to—well, compared to running loose, to being king of these mountains?" He tried a gentler tone, "You know, I used to hate him for stealing Red from me. But he must have looked on that a little different. He saw a fine mare that had been a mustang once, and he saw her bound up with all kinds of leather straps on. He must've thought he was breaking her out of jail by getting her away from me. Don't you see?"

She was silent for a long moment, her back turned to him. When she spoke her tone was despairing. "What would you do in my place?"

Rube sighed. "We're both in the same place, Abby. I think it's time we went home."

"And just leave him?"

"He's left us, Abby. We had him for a while. That much was a miracle, I reckon, some kind of miracle that we ever had him at all."

As she stared into the fire she looked close to tears. "I wish sometimes I'd never owned him."

"Yeah, but he wanted to! I mean, he let us ride him. He didn't have to, but he did. That's what bothers me. I don't know, but it seems like he was curious or something. He tasted all we had to offer, but I reckon now he was just visiting. Just visiting."

Abby sighed. "Next time remind me not to buy a visitor."

Rube nodded. "Next time."

"Do the men want to quit?"

"It's time," he told her. "It's time we all went home."

Chapter 17

———◆◆◆———

Rolling over in bed, Rube dreamed of the great black stallion rearing high in the sunset and pawing at the orange and purple sky, then whirling away to jump, to jump that chasm where the wind roared loud. The horse-hair lariat whooshed overhead. Rube threw hard as Shadow bounded for the edge. His loop reached out, gathered nothing. It brushed the stallion's mane, slid off his shiny back as Shadow launched himself . . . into space. Rube saw him falling away, away—

Rube sat up straight in bed, his heart thudding fast. For a moment that's all he could do, just sit there panting and waiting for his heart to slow down, while within him he tried to erase the vision of Shadow leaping to his death.

Just a dream, he told himself. Just a dream.

There was no use trying to go back to sleep. Dawn was brightening the curtains of his bedroom, so he got dressed and went outside. A horse was tied to the very end of the hitching rail near the front of the house.

Ambling toward it, he saw that the horse looked like

the one Hand-in-the-Fire rode sometimes. Then he spotted the lump of black fur in the corner of the front porch. Hand-in-the-Fire was curled up there with the Tucker watchdog. Dog lifted his head and peered out as Rube put his weight on the first creaking step. Some watchdog! The black bear hide stirred and Hand-in-the-Fire raised his head.

"Get here late?" Rube asked.

"Too early," Hand-in-the-Fire yawned. He looked as if he'd been riding all night. "Roki wants you. He says come quick."

"What for?"

"The one you call Shadow. We might have him soon." He sat all the way up then and gestured far to the north. "North of the Cloud Cascades. We run him for two weeks now. If we get him, Roki says your Barrett girl can have him for much money."

"North of—" Rube muttered, his eyes suddenly drawn to the distance. "So that's where they went. Is Firelight still leading?"

The Indian nodded. "She and Red."

"But Red doesn't know that ground. Does Firelight?"

Hand-in-the-Fire yawned in a way that sounded like "no" and stood up. "We ran them to place they don't know, but Roki does. They're lost and tired now. Roki says you should come."

"Sure thing," he said quickly. He started for the house and he twisted as he ran, calling back over his shoulder: "Help yourself to a fresh horse from that corral over there. I want to be there for the catch!"

He ran to wake up Pa and throw together the stuff they'd need. To his surprise, Pa didn't want to go. He didn't say why exactly, and he didn't try to talk Rube out of going. He just shook his head, looking tired and resigned. "You go on then," Pa said. "Roki's waiting."

"But don't you want to go?"

"Not this time."

"But this might be the last time!"

"I know," Pa said. "You go on now. Don't keep Roki waiting."

In a few minutes Rube and Hand-in-the-Fire were on their way.

Yet as they rode, Rube's nightmare kept coming back in ways that had to make him wonder. He'd heard of people dreaming about things that were actually happening somewhere else far away, so he had to wonder if Shadow had really jumped to his death that morning.

But no! He tried to shut out the thought.

They drove their horses hard for more than twenty miles, then changed horses at Roki's camp in the Cloud Cascades and rode on again with no break at all. Hand-in-the-Fire knew the way.

It was late afternoon before they found Roki's outfit. Rube felt worn to the bone, but excitement kept him going.

Roki was rushing to unsaddle his lathered horse when Rube arrived. The old man was still breathing hard from his last turn at chasing the wild ones. "We got him now," he panted. He motioned back toward a high rock mountain with hardly any trees on top. "Up there. Better change your horse."

"Then he's all right?" Rube asked.

"Better than me," Roki said, exhausted.

Rube climbed down and flapped back the stirrup to expose the cinch. One of the young Cheval boys was already leading over another horse for him, a line-backed mare. Rube kept glancing toward the mountain as he undid the cinch. "Up there? That one?"

Roki bobbed his head and pointed toward a narrow track that wound up the mountain. "We ran him until he tried that trail."

Rube threw the saddle to the ground for a moment and dug the brass telescope out of his saddlebags. "How many trails down?"

"No others." Roki looked to him with a tiny smile of satisfaction. "That is the only one."

Rube hesitated, surprised that Shadow could trap himself like that, but then, this wasn't Shadow's land. He couldn't know.

He stretched out the telescope, all its sections clicking into place in a fast zip, and peered at that trail. In a moment he found them high near the top—Shadow with four mares.

Slowly, he scanned the rest of the mountain. It was almost like a mesa, but it was not flat on top; it was more like a giant chunk of rock standing above the trees. Its summit rose at least four-hundred feet, long and rolling, like the back of a sleeping animal, but where the head should have been, a chasm cut the mountain in two. He studied that other chunk on the other side of the split. "Any trails over there on that other piece?"

"He can't jump it," Roki said. "No horse can."

"Even so, I've seen Shadow—"

"He cannot fly! That split is too wide. He would die."

"If he's cornered for sure," Rube said, "then let's take it easy. Let him figure out where he is and surrender. He surrendered before, when we finally had him good. He's no fool."

"And he knows you. He knows you'll treat him well."

Rube looked down, still kind of ashamed. "Well, he's Abby's now, but anyway we can't rush him."

"My braves know the danger. To all of us."

Rube closed up his telescope, stuffed it back in his saddlebag and buckled down the strap. "All right then. And about the reward. . ." He paused to put blanket and saddle on the fresh mare. "Divide it up any way you like. I don't want any of it."

"Just to follow him over the land." Roki smiled, knowing. "I thought your father would come."

"I thought so too, but he didn't want to. Don't know why."

"Maybe I do," Roki said, mounting up. "He's seen the great days of mustanging. Maybe he doesn't want to see the last."

They rode down to join Kehoni and the other Chevals who were guarding the trail up Shadow's mountain, and together they began the climb. Three braves led the way on foot. They carried stout poles and ropes in case they had to fight Shadow away from the trail's summit. Rube brought up the drag behind Roki and Kehoni and the other ten Chevals who were on horseback.

The path was narrow and steep, at times just a ledge which clung to the granite walls. Rube wished he was riding one of his own horses that he knew and could trust more. He'd never seen this one before. Her legs seemed to tremble as she followed the others with nervous care, at times pausing to watch the pebbles that rolled off the trail and fell away into silent distance.

"Easy there, easy," he whispered, then wondered if she understood any English at all.

Their trail angled and curved, making corners around sharp places where the world of pine trees lay far below. They came to a place where a piece of ledge had fallen away. One by one, Roki and the others urged their horses across. Rube grimaced as he watched them. And then it was his turn.

His mare stopped to sniff at the trail, to gawk at the wide-open distance below. But when Rube touched her sides with his boots, she stepped across with a little hop.

As they reached the summit, they caught sight of Firelight spying on them from atop a small rise. She dropped back out of sight then and ran back to Shadow. Kehoni looked after her with a tight-lipped expression. It wouldn't be long now. All the mustangs were out of sight beyond that rise.

The braves who came up on foot stayed back to guard the trailhead. With their poles they could fight back any mustangs that tried to get away down the path. Rube, Roki, Kehoni, and the other ten Chevals readied lariats.

As Rube shook out his loop, he fingered the bristly rope made of horsehair and prayed that once again it might do the job. His chest and throat felt squeezed, the awful tension of the moment binding him up. He looked to Roki and Kehoni and they smiled at one another in a knowing way. Rube signaled he was ready, so they started out.

Topping the last roll of bare rock, they looked down at the five wild horses trapped on the edge of the world. Shadow looked calm. Though he had to be exhausted, he still found the grit to carry himself like a lord of the wilderness, head up, tail up, nostrils wide.

Indians to the left and right moved up to form a close line of riders across the shelf. Then Roki signaled for them to stop.

When he did that, Shadow actually came forward, prancing with hooves springing high, with sure dignity in his bearing. Then he stopped and surveyed them like a king greeting guests in his palace. He looked at Rube with recognition.

Rube breathed easier, relieved that Shadow met them so calmly. But then the stallion's head turned, his atten-

tion caught by something, and Rube looked to see one
of the Indians shaking out a larger loop. Shadow's attention snapped back to Rube then, his gaze seeming as hard
and bitter as the day Rube had sold him to Abby. Once
again he looked betrayed.

Rube wilted as he understood something.

Shadow wasn't going back. Ever. It was in his eyes, in
the proud curve of his neck, the regal way he stood and
waited for these men to realize that he'd never go back
to man's ways. Here he was ruler of the high rocks. His
subjects followed him in a race against hunger and exhaustion, many until they couldn't go on any longer. Even
now four of them panted close by, among them Red and
Firelight, who were never going back either. Their legs
were shaking from weeks of hungry running, but they
huddled close, waiting for their stallion's next order. And
by the look in Shadow's eyes Rube could tell that he was
still their leader, still firmly in charge.

He wished Abby could see that look, could understand
that no amount of anybody's love could make any difference now. For Shadow'd had all that and now he'd made
his choice.

Rube found himself turning in the saddle as the Indians
began to move forward. He raised a hand and started to
tell Roki and the others to hold off and let them all go.
But at that moment Shadow shook his head, reared high
with a long whinny, and started for the edge.

"No," Rube told himself, then, "NO!" he screamed as
the nightmare lept inside him. "SHADOW!"

The stallion charged for the chasm that yawned too
wide, trying to throw his life at the shelf on the other side
which he had no chance of reaching.

If it hadn't been for that nightmare, for the terrible
knowing fear, he couldn't have moved, but the lariat was

already in his hand and he flinched to twirl it, to kick his pony closer. He sliced the air with his magic rope, cranked it three times and threw. The loop sailed out as the mares whinnied frantically.

For a sickening moment Rube thought he had missed. Then he saw the loop necktie and yanked rein, praying that Shadow wouldn't drag him over the edge. Before Shadow could leap, the rope yanked him back, almost jerked him over backward.

Roki's Indians hooted loudly at seeing the stallion lassoed and charged forward. Some rode to cut off the mares on one corner of the shelf, while others threw loops at Shadow. Two ropes missed, but two more caught his neck. Pebbles scattered over the edge as Shadow fought. He stood up on hind legs, squalling and pawing with blazing rage.

"Don't let him fall!" Rube yelled. "He'll drag us all down with him!" He dug heels into his pony, gritting his teeth against the yank of rope at the saddlehorn.

Three roping horses now worked to drag the fighting stallion away from the edge, yet suddenly Shadow stopped resisting and he attacked. He bolted at the nearest Indian with jaws wide and wolf teeth flashing.

Roki hollered in Cheval, and all the riders heeled their horses and wrenched back rein, spreading away from the stallion, holding him from every side as he lunged this way and that. When his mares whinnied to him from their corner on the shelf, it seemed to make him fight even harder.

Kehoni and Hand-in-the-Fire missed on their first throw and rushed to gather up their lariats to throw again. Hand-in-the-Fire's loop joined the others on Shadow's neck. Now they had four ropes on him.

Kehoni jumped from the saddle and ran forward, readying his loop as he went. He ducked under the straight ropes and got in close. Shadow kicked at him with hind legs, then reeled to stand and paw with forefeet. Kehoni edged nearer, almost under those black flint hooves, and he tossed his loop onto one of Shadow's forefeet. When it slipped tight, Kehoni changed direction and ran to the side, pulling the leg back under Shadow's body farther and farther until suddenly the great stallion went down and rolled over amid the whoops of the Indians. "Yea-Ha!"

As Shadow lay fighting to rise, Rube and Roki jumped to the ground and two-handed rope almost to within hoof and tooth range. "He almost died!" Rube shouted.

"We got him now," Roki grunted. "Kehoni, pull that way!"

"But he almost killed himself! Don't you see?"

"He can't now."

"But he won't live! He'll die!"

"Look out!" Roki yelled, as Shadow struck out at him with a sharp hoof. The ropes drew tighter around the stallion's throat, and Shadow started to wheeze, his windpipe closing.

"He's choking!" Rube shouted. "We're killing him, don't you see? We've got to let him go!"

Roki looked up, astonished. "Let him—"

"We've got to."

"Let him go?"

"Yes! He'll die right here if we don't."

Roki's gray braids flopped as he shook his head fast. "We can't.

"But we've got to! Look, we caught him. We always wanted to and we've done that. But we can't keep him! Look, if it's the money, I'll make it up to you. All of you. I'll give you what Abby would, but we've got to let him go."

Roki looked to the others and to Shadow, his eyes full of warning. "Too late, Rube Tucker." He flicked his eyes toward the stallion that kicked and struck and strangled between them. "He'd kill us now. He'd kill us all."

Rube held on, trying to see something beyond the wild-eyed fury that blazed from Shadow. Black hooves beat at the rocks. White teeth snapped. And with every creaking groan of the rope, the loops throttled tighter. Rube wagged his head. "It'd take a minute to kill us, wouldn't it? If he was loose, I don't think he'd waste the time."

Roki grunted doubtfully, but hesitated, weighing their chances for life or death. "Is it worth your life?"

"Maybe," Rube said. "Mine anyway."

Shadow began to wheeze louder, his eyes glazing over. As the Indians traded anxious looks, Kehoni looked desperate. "Maybe if he sees that his mares go free."

"His mares. Rube stared at him. "You mean Firelight, too?"

Kehoni bobbed his head just once, a quick nod. It had taken him years to capture Firelight, but he gave her away with a nod.

"Red, too, then," Rube said quickly. "Let 'em all go."

Roki let out a painful sigh, both his fists holding what he couldn't keep. "Too bad," he whispered, and then he called out in Cheval to the braves who guarded the mares. The Indians turned, unable to believe what they heard, but Roki yelled his order again even louder. He was telling them to let the mares go free.

Rube tried to thank him with a look, but Roki didn't glance at him. He took out his knife and inched closer to the stallion. The others took out knives too.

One brave helped hold tension on Rube's rope while he dug out his jackknife and pried open the blade. When he was ready, they crept closer along the ropes.

Rube wished he had lassoed Shadow with some other rope, for now he must cut his magic lariat. He had to hurry, for Shadow's wheezing grew more labored and his eyes were dimming.

"Together now," Rube whispered. "Up close . . .!"

It hurt to see his jackknife slice through that precious rope, through the many-colored hairs of horses he'd never forget, but it was over quickly and he jumped away.

Shadow's next struggling breath stretched open the ropes. He paused for a moment while his nostrils pulled wind and his eyes began to clear. Then suddenly he staggered up and shook his head to throw off the cut ropes. Firelight's whinny drew his attention. Seeing that she and Red and the other two mares were trotting toward him, free, he launched himself to them. He dashed between Rube and Roki without glancing at them as he ran to join his mares. One whinny sent them thundering off ahead of him, Red and Firelight in the lead. Once they were going, Shadow never looked back.

They galloped up the little rise and flowed away out of sight, headed down the mountain.

Still trembling, Rube felt almost too shaky to walk. The others were gathering at the cliff's rim, waiting for Shadow to come in sight down the mountainside again, so he went over to them. "Thanks," he told Roki. "I'll get your money on Saturday. I've got a thousand in the bank."

Roki only coiled up his lariat, dust on his spectacles. "You owe us nothing," he said.

"Nothing! But you worked so hard ."

"No more," the old man said. He looked to Kehoni then, a secret look that passed some meaning Rube couldn't read. "No more." And with that Roki stepped to the rim and gave a mighty heave, flinging his lariat out into space. It struck the ledge on the other side of the chasm that

Shadow had tried to jump and it spilled into coils, dropping out of sight.

Rube glanced down at his own lariat, knowing what Roki meant: it was over now. Mustanging as a way of life—it was all used up. The mountains were near cleaned out, and the barbed wire was coming. Maybe this way there would be something left—something of magic quality still remaining in the Winding Stairs.

Rube wound his lariat into a coil, letting his eyes wander from color to color, from memory to memory along that rope. He felt the hair and thought of all those horses, all those many mustangs caught and cared for and sold— now gone, except for this rope made of memories and hair.

This was the rope that caught Wild Shadow, twice in one lifetime, and now it was just about the most precious thing he had left. Yet he knew how to make the best use of it.

He gave it to the wind, just flung it away after Roki's with the hardest toss he could manage. It, too, rattled against the granite on the far side of the split and fell away.

"No more wild ones," he told them. "No more."

So they stood there at the edge, mustangers without ropes now, watching with a kind of joy as Shadow and Red and Firelight and the others came into view away down there. Running. Just running. Breezing over the rocks, rippling away until they were nothing but specks decorating the distance with graceful motion. There was no sound. Nothing but the swish of wind around the mountain, wind running loose to the land of Wild Shadow.

The Author

Zoltan Malocsay grew up on the outskirts of Miami, Oklahoma, "riding horses and flying airplanes." He graduated Phi Beta Kappa from the University of Oklahoma's School of Journalism and Professional Writing and did graduate work in Writer's Workshop courses at the University of Iowa. He has published numerous stories, reprinted in several textbooks. This is his first novel.
several textbooks. This is his first novel.

Mr. Malocsay is also a sculptor-goldsmith whose one-of-a-kind creations are sold to galleries in the West. He and his English wife live currently in Colorado.